Enchanted

Also from Lexi Blake

ROMANTIC SUSPENSE

Masters and Mercenaries
The Dom Who Loved Me
The Men With The Golden Cuffs
A Dom is Forever
On Her Master's Secret Service
Sanctum: A Masters and Mercenaries Novella
Love and Let Die
Unconditional: A Masters and Mercenaries Novella
Dungeon Royale
Dungeon Games: A Masters and Mercenaries Novella
A View to a Thrill
Cherished: A Masters and Mercenaries Novella
You Only Love Twice
Luscious: Masters and Mercenaries~Topped
Adored: A Masters and Mercenaries Novella
Master No
Just One Taste: Masters and Mercenaries~Topped 2
From Sanctum with Love
Devoted: A Masters and Mercenaries Novella
Dominance Never Dies
Submission is Not Enough
Master Bits and Mercenary Bites~The Secret Recipes of Topped
Perfectly Paired: Masters and Mercenaries~Topped 3
For His Eyes Only
Arranged: A Masters and Mercenaries Novella
Love Another Day
At Your Service: Masters and Mercenaries~Topped 4
Master Bits and Mercenary Bites~Girls Night
Nobody Does It Better
Close Cover
Protected: A Masters and Mercenaries Novella
Enchanted: A Masters and Mercenaries Novella

Masters and Mercenaries: The Forgotten
Lost Hearts (Memento Mori)
Lost and Found
Lost in You, Coming August 6, 2019

Lawless
Ruthless
Satisfaction
Revenge

Courting Justice
Order of Protection
Evidence of Desire

Masters Of Ménage (by Shayla Black and Lexi Blake)
Their Virgin Captive
Their Virgin's Secret
Their Virgin Concubine
Their Virgin Princess
Their Virgin Hostage
Their Virgin Secretary
Their Virgin Mistress

The Perfect Gentlemen (by Shayla Black and Lexi Blake)
Scandal Never Sleeps
Seduction in Session
Big Easy Temptation
Smoke and Sin
At the Pleasure of the President

URBAN FANTASY

Thieves
Steal the Light
Steal the Day
Steal the Moon
Steal the Sun
Steal the Night

Ripper
Addict
Sleeper
Outcast

LEXI BLAKE WRITING AS SOPHIE OAK

Small Town Siren
Siren in the City
Away From Me
Three to Ride
Siren Enslaved
Two to Love
Siren Beloved
One to Keep
Siren in Waiting
Lost in Bliss
Found in Bliss
Siren in Bloom
Pure Bliss
Chasing Bliss
Siren Unleashed

Enchanted

A Masters and Mercenaries Novella

By Lexi Blake

1001 Dark Nights

EVIL EYE

CONCEPTS

Enchanted
A Masters and Mercenaries Novella
By Lexi Blake

1001 Dark Nights

Published by Evil Eye Concepts, Incorporated

Acknowledgments from the Author

This year has been a journey for me. After I lost my mother the previous July, I was told to give it a year to sink in. I'll be honest I've been numb most of the year. I've gone through my days marking time and writing words and only feeling what I put on the page. I got into a routine. Then I took a trip that changed things. I had planned this trip for way over a year and when it finally came around, I didn't want to go. I'm glad I did because I realized what I had been missing in the last year. Wonder.

Thank you to RARE Paris for giving me a reason to go.

Thank you to MJ and Kristen for making me understand that I am not alone in my grief.

Thank you to Jillian who boldly led us to places she didn't even want to go.

Thank you to Kim for taking care of my baby girl so I could explore Munich.

Thank you to my husband for taking his bad knees up into the Alps and never complaining.

Thank you to my daughter for letting me see the world through her eyes.

Thank you to Steve for letting me share an amazing journey.

Thank you to Liz for holding my hand and taking me up a mountain and for helping me find my wonder again.

But in the end this book is dedicated to one of the best friendships I've ever seen. To Kori and Sara. I wish you all the happily ever afters and I'm deeply proud to be considered your friend.

Sign up for the 1001 Dark Nights Newsletter
and be entered to win a Tiffany Key necklace.

There's a contest every month!

Go to www.1001DarkNights.com to subscribe.

**As a bonus, all subscribers can download
FIVE FREE exclusive books!**

One Thousand and One Dark Nights

Once upon a time, in the future...

*I was a student fascinated with stories and learning.
I studied philosophy, poetry, history, the occult, and
the art and science of love and magic. I had a vast
library at my father's home and collected thousands
of volumes of fantastic tales.*

*I learned all about ancient races and bygone
times. About myths and legends and dreams of all
people through the millennium. And the more I read
the stronger my imagination grew until I discovered
that I was able to travel into the stories... to actually
become part of them.*

*I wish I could say that I listened to my teacher
and respected my gift, as I ought to have. If I had, I
would not be telling you this tale now.
But I was foolhardy and confused, showing off
with bravery.*

*One afternoon, curious about the myth of the
Arabian Nights, I traveled back to ancient Persia to
see for myself if it was true that every day Shahryar
(Persian: شهریار, "king") married a new virgin, and then
sent yesterday's wife to be beheaded. It was written
and I had read, that by the time he met Scheherazade,
the vizier's daughter, he'd killed one thousand
women.*

Something went wrong with my efforts. I arrived in the midst of the story and somehow exchanged places with Scheherazade — a phenomena that had never occurred before and that still to this day, I cannot explain.

Now I am trapped in that ancient past. I have taken on Scheherazade's life and the only way I can protect myself and stay alive is to do what she did to protect herself and stay alive.

Every night the King calls for me and listens as I spin tales. And when the evening ends and dawn breaks, I stop at a point that leaves him breathless and yearning for more. And so the King spares my life for one more day, so that he might hear the rest of my dark tale.

As soon as I finish a story... I begin a new one... like the one that you, dear reader, have before you now.

Prologue

In which we meet our fairy godparents and hope they don't cuss too much…

Charlotte Taggart felt the baby fluttering in her belly and a deep sense of peace filled her. She genuinely enjoyed being pregnant. It wasn't for everyone. Her sister hated it, and Simon was going to have to be happy with the only kiddo he would ever share with Chelsea. Her friend Kori had vowed to never be pregnant, and it worked for her and Kai. They had a whole lot of dogs and it filled the need for them. The truth was there was no one way to have a family.

But damn she loved hers—all of them. She loved the ones she shared blood with and the ones she'd chosen. She was blessed beyond measure.

It made her feel the need to give back.

Soft baby snuffles came from the monitor, letting her know her son was still sleeping. She'd given up keeping a monitor in the twins' room since they'd gotten big enough to simply come and ask for what they needed. Too many times she overheard plans for world domination and it kept her up at night.

The son in her stomach twisted again, but it wasn't anywhere close to uncomfortable yet. That was still months away. For now, his kicks felt like waves across her belly.

Soft light illuminated the kitchen and she couldn't help but think about how far she'd come from the child she'd been. Moscow didn't have many sunny days, but here in Dallas the light seemed to always be around her.

Light and love and laughter.

"He giving you hell, baby?" The question rumbled against the nape of her neck and she was pulled back against the hard planes of her husband's body. He'd gone to bed wearing nothing at all, but she knew he would have slid his strong legs into pajama bottoms or sweat pants before he'd left the room. His chest, however, was still warm and bare. "You're up early. Or were you trying to sneak in some quiet time before the monsters awaken?"

Nothing ever felt as good as that moment when Ian took her in his arms. And he was right. She loved her three kiddos. Kenzie and Kala and Seth. Soon there would be four, and she wasn't so foolish as to believe her baby girls wouldn't immediately start training their youngest brother in how to take on the parents. But that wasn't what had gotten her out of bed. "I was plotting."

She could feel him smile against her shoulder, where he was currently laying soft kisses and getting her hot and bothered. He pushed her hair to the side to give himself better access.

"I love it when you plot. Is this a bloody, take-no-prisoners plot where I get to murder people? Because it's been a long time." His hands moved up to cup her breasts.

Murder did tend to get her man hot, but alas, she had different plans. "Did you hear the rumors about Sarah?"

He went still and she found herself turned around, his forehead touching hers. "I did. We're not supposed to talk about it. She only told Wade because he needed to know why she won't be working her shifts in the nursery. Wade only mentioned it to me because I'm the boss and I would notice. I think the girls will notice, too. They love Sarah. How did you find out?"

"I snooped," she admitted.

"Charlie." He sometimes managed to turn her name into an admonition, but she was made of sterner stuff. She'd worked for the mafia for years. She could handle some shame.

"I overheard her in the locker room talking to her doctor on the phone. She didn't know anyone was there. She's wrong to keep this a secret." Years of working for her mafia father had proven to her that real family meddled in the nicest of ways. Not in the "hey, go kill this guy in Italy" way. In the "we don't want you to be alone even though you think you should be" way.

"I'm sure she thinks it's for the best, though I don't know why she doesn't want people to know. It's nothing to be ashamed of," Ian said.

But Charlie understood. "It's not, but it feels like it is. You can't understand, but you can help."

"All right. How do we help her?"

Tears pierced her eyes because this was what she loved about him. Ian Taggart. Big, mean, sarcastic, kind. "We can't fix her problem, but did you know Jared is coming into town and he's asked for access to the club?"

Jared John Ferguson, Hollywood hottie and little brother of Sanctum's resident psychologist, Kai. For Sarah Stevens, Jared was the one who got away. At least initially he had. He'd changed his mind after a few months. He'd been trying to work his way back into her life, but she'd been burned one too many times before. She wouldn't let him back in. Not without a push. Luckily, Charlotte was good at being pushy.

Ian lifted his head and sharp blue eyes stared down at her. "What are you planning, my gorgeous brat, and how can I work it so it also includes a terrible prank on Adam?"

She rolled her eyes. "You need to be nicer to him."

He thought about it for a moment and then nodded. "That could work. Throw him off a little. God, you're brilliant, baby. He'll be incredibly paranoid at the end of it. Let's send flowers to the new office. He'll lose his shit trying to figure out what's wrong with them. This is awesome."

She reached for him. If she let him, he would spend the whole day fixated on the best flowers to send Adam into a tidal wave of paranoia. "I was talking about playing matchmaker for Sarah and Jared."

"I can do both," he insisted. "Do you think with everything going on in Sarah's life that now is the time for Jared to come on strong?"

Jared had done a television show called *Dart* for years before the show had been canceled. He'd had a brief flirtation with Sarah Stevens, but after being arrested for murder and discovering that his best friend was actually a serial killer, he'd gone away to get his head on straight.

Sarah had not been happy about being left behind.

"If not now, when? Come on, it's kind of romantic, right? And I hate the thought of her going through this alone."

"You're giving me puppy eyes," he sighed. "I can't resist those. Tell me what you're thinking and how we avoid the inevitable bloody ending, because it somehow always happens. We go into a plot trying to bring two idiots who can't see how perfect they are for each other together and suddenly the bullets start flying."

"There's no reason for bullets to fly this time. None." She'd been more than happy with the calm they'd had for the last couple of months. Sure there had been that super-fun time in Colorado, but she and Ian hadn't been the ones dodging bullets. She liked being a distraction, especially when it included a couple of nights in a really nice nudist resort where she'd very likely conceived this baby boy. "But we could help two people who love each other find their way into each other's arms."

Ian stepped back, putting a hand on his washboard abs and grimacing. "Now you're giving *me* morning sickness, Charlie."

"You know what I'm saying. They need a little push."

"And how are you going to push them?" His eyes had gone warm as though he was excited to hear what she had planned.

She'd been up for a while now thinking it through. It had been a long time since the group had a big blowout. "Well, my birthday is coming up in a few days. I was thinking a wildly over-the-top weekend event at Sanctum is exactly what I need."

He put his hands on his hips and smiled at her. "Well, you are the queen of that particular kingdom. I take it you have a plan for this over-the-top event."

"I do. I just need you to help me out."

"As you wish, my love." He pulled her close. "Now tell me what you want."

She smiled because the plan could wait. She went on her toes and told her man exactly what she wanted.

Him.

Chapter One

In which our erstwhile hero speaks to his brother...and his brother calls him a moron.

Jared Johns settled into the comfy chair in his brother's office and hoped that his choice of seat didn't give Kai a reason to start psychoanalyzing him. There really hadn't been another choice. He kind of thought Kai liked it that way.

"You haven't worked in a while," Kai said, sitting across from him. "How does that make you feel?"

Jared sighed. It wouldn't have mattered if he'd refused to sit down. His big brother was a shrink and he psychoanalyzed absolutely everyone. "It makes me feel glad I invested wisely. I did not come here to ask for cash. I'm good."

Kai sent him a perfectly innocent look. "I wasn't implying you came to ask for a loan, Jared. You were on a popular TV show for years. Your last movie part fell through. It's got to be rough, but you don't talk about it."

There were reasons he didn't talk about his career with his sainted brother. Kai had gone into the military after their mother died and sent back everything he could to support his baby brother. It wasn't his fault their aunt hadn't actually given him the cash. Kai had been the one to work his way to a doctorate. Kai was the one who lived a simple life, treating patients with profound PTSD for almost no money at all. Jared had been the one funding him for the last couple of years, though they'd agreed to keep that quiet.

And he was okay with that because Jared was the one who ran around in spandex and leather pretending to be a superhero. He was the brother known for whole YouTube channels devoted to his workouts.

"I wish you would talk about it," Kai said. "I know the last few years had to have been difficult. The show was important to you."

It had been everything at one point in time. It had been his ticket to a new life. Now it was hard to think about what his dream job had cost others. "Well, it was apparently my fault *Dart* got canceled."

Kai settled his glasses on his nose and sat back. "I don't see how. You got even better at throwing darts around over the years. Your abs stayed tight. I don't know what happened."

Yes, this was why he didn't talk to his brother about his job woes. "The last two seasons' storylines sucked. The head writer blamed me because his fiancée left him and he tanked the show by sending Dart to jail and making the whole thing into a political statement on the way prisoners are treated."

Kai nodded. "Yes, I liked that part."

"I was sent to Stankfield Prison. No one names a prison that." It had been the single worst year of his life. He'd rapidly learned the power he had with the producer. None. He was supposed to shut up, read his lines, and not get pudgy.

"You also managed to fashion darts out of any number of things no one can fashion darts out of."

"I get that you didn't like the show." His brother was an overly pretentious intellectual. "I didn't come here to fight with you. I also didn't come to have a session."

Kai leaned over. "I wasn't trying to fight. I guess I'm not sure how to talk to you. I'm worried about you. I know you made some money from the show, but that place out in Malibu has to be expensive. And I know you were counting on that racing film."

Ah, there was the man who'd pretty much raised him. Jared couldn't even blame him. He'd been a fuckup most of his life. His brother didn't get that he'd gotten his shit together. "Money is not a problem and honestly, the acting thing I can take or leave at this point. The movie fell through because Josh Hunt hurt his back doing a stunt and they recast the role. When he was no longer doing the film, they suddenly didn't want me."

Josh had been his best friend for the last couple of years. Josh had stood by him even when it wasn't great for his career to do so. Even when the world had been questioning whether or not Jared Johns had something to do with his oldest friend's hobby.

Kai stared at him for a moment as though trying to decide how to continue. "Are you sure the lack of work isn't due to the social media stuff?"

"I'm sure it played its part." Social media. It was funny how much it had helped him on his way up. He would post a work-out video and get a couple million views. At one point he'd been one of the most followed people in social media. He still had a ton of fans, but he'd discovered the dark side to the web. Not the nasty assholes who came on and told him he should shut up about whatever cause he was trying to help, or the ones who called him arrogant and ugly. He could deal with those people. There was another group. The trolls were the people who sniffed blood and pounced. They caught on to a conspiracy theory and remade reality into a horrible place.

"Have you thought about suing?" Kai's mouth went tight. "Because I have. I've thought about suing a couple of the fuckers."

They got on his social media and called him a killer. They spread rumors that he'd killed Squirrel to cover up his own crimes, that he'd been the one to murder those women. It didn't matter that the police had cleared him. In their world, he paid off witnesses and apparently owned the cops. In their world he would always be guilty and they would protest anyone who hired him. "What good would it do? If I get one blocked, another twelve show up, and it's probably the same one I blocked in the first place, coming back at me under another name. Social media is anonymous. People can get on and say things they would never say in real life. There's not a lot I can do about it except continue to be me and not let them drag me into the muck."

"Or you could let some of your brother's friends use their talents to find the little fuckers and teach them a lesson."

Sometimes he forgot how bloodthirsty Kai could be. He always seemed civilized. He always had been, but there was a dark side to his brother. There was a side that had done well in the Army, that likely would have led to an excellent career there if he hadn't been so unwilling to indulge that sadistic part of his personality. Kai knew how dark he could get and he managed it, feeding his beast in the best of ways. It didn't hurt that he'd found the one woman on earth who could complete him.

"I appreciate that, but it wouldn't solve the problem." The fact that his brother wanted to protect him, to avenge him, settled something deep inside Jared.

"Then what will?" Kai visibly calmed himself. It was something he'd seemed to always be able to do, to turn aside the dark impulses and find his peaceful center. "Because I'm worried you won't be able to work with all this negativity around you. I know the show aged and it had a good run, but I also think it would have lasted a few more seasons if the scandal hadn't happened."

A lot of things would have lasted had Squirrel not turned out to be a raging psychopath, and the least of those was his career. He needed to put his brother's mind at ease. "Kai, I'm worth a hundred million. I made a lot of money in the last couple of years doing endorsements overseas. *Dart* was big over there. I still make money doing appearances. I invested most of what I made in the last few seasons. I lived in Vancouver and didn't spend a dime I didn't have to. I bought the place in Malibu with cash. I produced a couple of films that did really well."

The lack of acting work hurt, but he'd learned the game pretty quickly. He'd figured out who his friends were and who had been hanging out to get ahead. His movie career as an actor seemed blocked and he might have missed his chance. He could find a TV gig. He'd been offered a couple despite the crap that still clung to him. Television was where the industry had slotted him. He could go back to working eighty-hour weeks and not seeing anyone outside the cast and crew. That had been enough for him in the beginning. He'd been beloved. The fans had been crazy about him. He'd gotten something from the hype surrounding the show.

He needed more now.

"Well, you have a hundred million dollars, so who the fuck cares?" His brother said the words with a sort of hushed awe that had Jared grinning.

It was good to know he could still shock his brother. Though in a good way this time. "Fuck 'em. I'm fine on the work front. I've got a couple of projects in pre-production. The real money is in producing, and I've got great ties in the sci-fi world. I want to run some ideas by Kori while I'm here."

Kai's wife was a brilliant screenwriter. So brilliant she'd been smart enough to leave LA. Not that he hated LA. He loved parts of it. He just hated the part where he was already seen as a washed-up loser because he wasn't in a blockbuster film. There were other ways to have a career.

"I'm surprised. I guess I thought you would find another show after *Dart*."

He didn't fault Kai for thinking that way. After all, he'd spent the majority of his life seeking attention—good or bad. But he'd grown up. "I need something more. I know you think the acting thing was all about narcissism…"

Kai shook his head. "Hey, that is not what I think at all. I do not in any way think you're a narcissist. Quite the opposite. You're kind, Jared. You think of others. I might have had a lot of baggage when it comes to you, but the last couple of years have shown me what a good person you are. But your personality type requires positive reinforcement."

It was how he'd gotten in trouble so many times. He knew what Kai saw when he looked at his younger brother. Their father had walked out on them when they were young. Kai had taken over much of the protector role while their mother had worked and worked to keep food on the table. Jared had gone from his mom walking him to school every day and being the room mom, tirelessly showing up on the sidelines of whatever sport he was playing that month, to almost never seeing her at all. He'd needed the attention, and looking for it had almost led to losing his whole family.

He knew one thing now. "I've tried to fill that void with fans, and it doesn't work because not one of them knows the real me. I think for a long time I loved acting because I didn't have to be me at all. I had to be whatever character I was playing, and then offscreen I was the actor Jared Johns. I didn't have to be Jared Ferguson."

Because Jared Ferguson had been a scared kid. He'd been a fucked-up kid. He'd been selfish and self-centered and lost and so vulnerable it hurt to think about it.

"You want to be Jared Ferguson again?" Kai asked.

"It's taken me a while but yes. I think that's what's come out of all of this, out of what happened with Squirrel." This was the part his brother might not like. "I mentioned I'm making a documentary."

"I know. I think it's a good way to examine what happened to you."

Jared breathed a sigh of relief. He'd been worried his brother would have reservations, and the documentary was absolutely nonnegotiable. "Good. We've done the background work on Squirrel and where he came from, how he turned into what he did."

A killer. Squirrel had been his oldest friend, someone who'd had his back since childhood. It was still hard to think of the things he'd done.

"I was hoping you would consent to talk about the incident on screen." He was cautious, knowing he was tiptoeing into a field of landmines where his brother was concerned. Kai was a deeply private individual. "I thought you could talk about things from a psychological perspective."

His brother's lips turned down in a prissy frown, though he was sure Kai would object to the word. "I don't like to go on camera. That's not what I do."

He nodded and waved it off like he'd known that would be the reaction. Which he had. "No problem. I thought that's what you might say. I wanted to give you first dibs. I've got another psychologist lined up. Kenny Prewitt. He's done a couple of documentaries on true crime. Don't worry about it."

Kai's face immediately went a nice shade of red. "That quack? You can't be serious. He's not a real psychologist. He's a nice head of hair. That's all I can say about that idiot."

Jared let Kai rant on. He'd known Kenny Prewitt had a long history of clashing with Kai. They'd been in the same doctoral program. Kai had gone into private practice and Ken had found fame as the therapist to the stars.

Dr. Kenny wasn't actually doing the documentary. There was no way he was paying what Dr. Kenny asked, and Kai was right about him being nothing more than a good haircut and some really shockingly white veneers that could be hard on his cinematography. But Kai didn't have to know that.

"I'll do it." Kai pronounced the words with a sigh like he'd known he would have to bail his little brother out again.

Yeah, score one for the actor. "That's great, Kai. You were actually there. You're the one who was involved. I think your input could be invaluable."

Kai frowned. "That doesn't mean I should talk about it on camera."

Jared shrugged. "Dr. Kenny said it might not be good for you. He said you're probably too close to the subject to be able to talk about it. He had some theories about you he was more than willing to share."

"I will share my theories with him. I will share them right up his probably bleached asshole, and then we'll see how he feels," Kai vowed.

"Oh, he's out if you're in. I just need someone who can talk about the incident from a psychological point of view." And that person had always been Kai. He had to be sneaky about making sure Kai said yes.

"Fine. I suppose I'll have to do it. Are you planning on talking to the other people who were affected?"

"I already have talked to them. That part of the documentary was the most important. It was hard. I talked to each of the victims' families." He had to look away or Kai would see how haunted he still was. "It wouldn't be right if I simply told his story and not theirs."

"Why wouldn't you tell me you were seeing the families? I would have come with you to make sure you're all right. Those women, they were murdered because Squirrel had an obsession with you. A rational person would understand that doesn't mean you're at fault."

"But a father whose daughter was killed because she'd had a brief affair with a TV star isn't rational." He had to take a deep breath. "It was terrible and I had to do it. It wasn't until I showed him how I intended to portray Carrie that he even would meet with me. Mia had to talk to him."

Mia Taggart had been involved. She'd had a friend who'd died at Squirrel's hands. At the time she'd thought it was Jared himself doing the killing, crawling across the world like a spider finding his next victim.

The film was as much about Jared's own blindness as it was Squirrel's evil.

Mia had built a bridge between Jared and the victims' families. She'd convinced them he would do the right thing by their daughters and sisters. He meant to make her proud.

"I don't cut myself slack," he admitted. "I knew something was wrong with Squirrel. I knew something was up with the way he treated women, but he was my buddy. Surely he was just blowing off steam. I didn't think there was any way he could hurt one of them. I want this to be a wake-up call. Men…we can't let other men off the hook when it comes to this. I know it's an extreme case, but what would have happened if I'd taken it seriously the first time he catcalled a woman or talked about how he wanted to strangle the ones who nagged too much?"

Kai sent him a sympathetic look. "If I were in your place, I likely would have thought he was joking, too."

"No, you would have known. You would have asked the pertinent questions. Kai, it's okay. Part of making this whole documentary is about taking responsibility. I can't forgive myself until I truly know the wrong I did. I think you told me that once." He'd learned a lot from his brother. He'd learned that sometimes a man had to be patient. And sometimes patience didn't work and a man had to press things forward a bit. "Now let's talk about the other thing I need from you."

"An invitation to Sanctum?" Kai asked, his lips curling up in a knowing smile.

There was a reason he needed the invitation. He'd run away from a lot of things when he'd left Dallas last time. "I gave up my membership when I walked away from Sarah."

Kai studied him for a moment. "You're ready to try this again?"

"I know she doesn't want to talk to me, but she agreed to do the documentary. That has to mean something. I won't hurt her. If she chooses to not play with me, I'll probably go home and I won't bother her again. She spoke to me on the phone a couple of months back about the project."

"I'm surprised she didn't mention it to me." Kai was married to Sarah's best friend. They were deeply entrenched in each other's daily lives.

"I suspect she's embarrassed." He'd thought for a long time about why Sarah wouldn't forgive him. "For a couple of months, we regularly talked. And then she stopped all of a sudden."

"She stopped returning your calls?" Kai asked. "That doesn't sound like Sarah. She's not afraid of confrontation. What happened the last time you talked to her?"

He'd gone over it again and again. He'd replayed that phone call a thousand times in his head. "We talked about her day. She'd worked a long shift because of a massive traffic accident. She wanted me to tell her stories about celebrities I've met. I think she found that soothing. Especially the ones where they turn out to be assholes, and that's a surprising number of them."

"I do not find that surprising at all," Kai replied. "So you two didn't argue?"

"No. We were even doing something together. We bought those DNA tests, the ones that tell you where you come from." It had been a silly thing to do, but they'd spit in the little vial together one night, making fun of each other over a video chat. She'd teased him telling him she was way better at swallowing. They'd been moving forward. "We were betting on who was going to have the more boring ancestry."

"And then she refused to talk to you?"

"I was gone for three weeks filming in Asia. It's a streaming movie that comes out next summer. We were in a pretty remote spot and I wasn't able to keep in touch. But I'd told her I would call her when I got back. I was going to ask her to come out and see me. I thought we'd gotten to be friendly again and maybe it was time to move into something more. I'd cleaned up my personal life entirely. You remember my friend, the one I pretended to date to keep the press off both of us? Well, I explained I couldn't do it anymore because I needed Sarah to understand she would be the only woman in my life. I was going to explain this to her but when I got back to the States, she refused to take my calls."

"Something happened," Kai mused. "Recently. She's been quieter than normal. When I ask, she simply smiles and tells me nothing's wrong and I'm being too 'shrinky,' as she puts it. That is not a technical term, by the way."

But it sounded very much like a Sarah term. She was utterly adorable. "She finally replied to an email I sent about the documentary. She agreed to do the interview but she demanded more cash and asked that I not call her again until it was time to film. I don't understand. She seemed like she was getting over it."

"Getting over you dumping her?" Kai asked in that tone that let him know he'd said something stupid. "You know that's a dumbass move when you're in love with a woman. She tends to take exception."

He'd had his reasons. They'd seemed like good ones at the time. "I had just found out my friend was a killer and that she'd been his next victim. I had to watch him die. He deserved it, but he was still a big part of my life. Yeah, I needed a time-out. But that doesn't mean I don't still want her. It doesn't mean I don't think about her every minute of the day. I've been celibate. I haven't touched another woman since before I met her."

Two and a half years. He hadn't had sex in two and a half years. Before he'd met Sarah he hadn't gone two weeks without. The problem was he knew she was the one and he couldn't cheat on her. If he had any shot at winning her back, at showing her they could work, he had to be serious about their relationship. Even when it didn't exist.

Kai was staring at him with something akin to awe. "Are you serious?"

Jared nodded. "I'm in love with her. It's wrong to sleep with someone else. This is my last shot. If she can't find a way to forgive me for walking out the first time, then I'll try to move on. But I want this chance with her."

"Well, it's your lucky day because Ian Taggart called before you came in and wanted me to put together Doms and subs for this big party thing he's throwing for Charlotte's birthday…of course. How does he see these things before I do? He knew you were in town, right?"

Big Tag had been one of his first calls. "I asked him if we could do some filming in the building since it's part of the story."

"He's a smart asshole. Well, brother, looks like you get your chance."

Jared breathed a sigh of relief as Kai started to explain. This was his shot and he was taking it.

Chapter Two

In which our heroine receives an invitation to the ball...

"What do you think it means? Is Charlotte seriously having a birthday party that lasts three days? That's pretty legit." Sarah Stevens stared down at the beautifully engraved invitation that had been dropped off at her apartment earlier in the day. "Did you get one?"

She stood in front of her locker at Sanctum, still wearing her scrubs. It had been a long shift and she was looking forward to some play. She wished she was looking forward to some crazy sex, but that wasn't happening.

Of course Jared Johns was in town. He was precisely the reason she hadn't had any freaky sex in a very long time. The idea of calling him up whispered across her mind. She could sleep with him, spend the weekend in bed with him, and then he would be gone. It wasn't like she was taking any big risks. He would go back to his Hollywood life and she would…she would do what she had to do. No muss. No fuss.

She would do it in a heartbeat if she truly thought he would walk away. If she thought she could swipe some sweetness from his super-gorgeous honey pot and get away clean, she would be in bed with him now. Screw playing in the club. They could do it privately and she could spend her last weekend doing nasty, filthy glorious things to that man's hot bod. But he claimed he wanted more.

And she'd so recently learned she didn't have more to give.

"I did. Apparently the queen has decided to have a royal ball in celebration of her birthday," Kori said with a grin. "I've heard it's going to be three nights of crazy games including a capture fantasy event when our Doms get to hunt us down, and the longer we stay free the more pleasure they owe us."

Sarah frowned. "That doesn't seem fair. Some of the subs are also former CIA. I'm a trauma nurse. I'm not allowed to hide from anything."

Of course, she'd also earned the nickname "Dateline" from her high school classmates who'd decided she was the one most likely to end up the victim portion of a *Dateline* episode. She couldn't help it if she had a trusting heart. She'd really thought that guy had a puppy in his car. It wasn't her fault he'd been running a sex trafficking ring and hey, she'd been the one to Tase him, and that led the police to shutting the whole thing down, so who was *Dateline* now?

"I don't think it's a real competition," Kori replied. "That could get hardcore fast. I think this is more of a metaphor."

"Don't count on it," a husky voice said, a chuckle flavoring her words. Eve McKay had the locker across from Sarah's. "I saw Charlotte studying the plans for the building. Specifically the air ducts. She's crazy if she thinks she can still get through those. It should be a super-fun night, but Kori's right about the pleasure part. I, for one, am going to let Alex find me immediately so we can get to the privacy rooms while they're still open."

"Smart," Kori pointed out. "Capture fantasy makes Kai's dick go crazy."

She wanted someone's dick to go crazy for her. Didn't she deserve that? "What about the unattached subs? Are we just running around the club hoping some unattached Dom decides he wants to catch us? What if I don't want to be caught by the guy who catches me?"

"Yeah, I don't think Big Tag's going to let that happen," a new voice said. Avery O'Donnell strode to her locker followed by Serena Dean-Miles. "That would be super chaotic, and then the Doms get territorial and pissy and fistfights start."

"And Ian doesn't want that?" Serena asked, a brow rising over her eyes. "Because he is the man who started up Dom Fight Club."

"It's different when the ladies are involved," Avery pointed out. "He'll laugh all day long when some man who thinks he can still fight like he did when he was twenty takes a punch from Boomer, who seriously doesn't know how hard he hits, but he would flip out if it happened to one of the women."

Serena frowned. "How is Li's back?"

"Pushing forty and not recovering the way it used to." Still, Avery smiled. "I think he'll think twice before taking on the young guns again. At least in a non-sneaky way. But I heard they've been pairing unattached Doms and subs for the weekend party."

So she would be paired with someone she probably knew well and wouldn't want to sleep with at all. Not because they weren't hot, but because she'd known those guys for years and if something was going to happen, it already would have. She'd played with every Dom in the place. Maybe she should think about this. She only had a couple of days left and she wanted to have fun. If she didn't have it at Sanctum, she should have it on her own. Who did she know who would know male hookers? Did they still call them gigolos? What was the proper terminology? She didn't want to insult one.

Kori turned around, giving Sarah her back and thereby access to the ties of her corset. "Do me a solid Scarlett O'Hara, please. And tell me why you have your fretting face on. You're going on vacay next week, right?"

She was taking a whole bunch of days off, but she definitely wouldn't call it a vacay. Not that she was letting anyone else know. She would tell them afterward. When she knew. "I'm not fretting. I just have a lot to do before I leave and I'm wondering if I shouldn't skip the festivities. I know all the Doms. My capture fantasy will end with a dude who's like my brother tackling me and probably giving me noogies."

It was not the way she'd wanted to spend this last weekend.

"Kai told me a couple of the MT guys recently got Master rights. You haven't met them. Also, a couple of single Doms from The Club are joining in," Serena pointed out. "And Michael is bringing his super-hot brother, JT, with him."

"They're twins," Eve pointed out. "Aren't they both super hot?"

"I know Michael way too well to think of him as hot," Serena replied. "JT has the cowboy thing going on. Not that I don't prefer my two big-city hotties. Also, does anyone know why Ian sent a big bouquet of flowers to the office today? Was it someone's birthday? Adam's being paranoid about it. Jake had to prove to him the flowers weren't bugged, and by that I mean both ways. Like they weren't actively spying on the office, nor did they contain a fleet of DNA enhanced superbugs that would attack him later."

Adam had a vivid imagination. But Serena had a point about new

Doms.

Was she really going to ignore the fact that Jared was in town and she was supposed to spend a couple of days working with him? She wouldn't if she didn't need the money he'd offered.

She gripped Kori's laces and gave them a good tug.

That part about the money probably wasn't true. She would have done the documentary money or not since it might bring her some closure. She and Jared had gotten close in those first days when he'd come to Dallas to spend time with his brother and prep for a movie role. She truly hadn't expected to fall for Jared Johns. She had thought a brief affair would be nice, and then she could forever say she'd slept with Dart and hit a total bullseye.

Yeah, she wasn't proud she'd thought that.

Then she'd gotten to know the actual man and not the beefcake actor. She'd wondered if maybe they might have something. The rest could have easily served as the plot of a horror film. His bestie had tried to murder her. Jared had saved her. Jared had left her.

Now he was back and he wanted to examine what had happened.

At least it wasn't *Dateline*.

"He really thinks Ian has access to superbugs?" Eve asked in that "maybe we should have a couple of sessions" way.

Eve was a therapist. It was a minus in Sarah's book since they took sanity very seriously, and she'd learned that definition was not always the same for all people. She pulled the laces through again, making them even before giving another tug that had Kori huffing.

"Don't be a baby." They still had a long way to go with those laces.

"Babies like to breathe," Kori complained. "At least that's what I remember about my babyhood. Breathing was kind of a thing."

Then she shouldn't have decided to wear a corset. "You can pay me back in a minute."

"Then you're staying? Because you had that 'I'm running away' look in your eyes."

Kori apparently spent a lot of time evaluating her expressions. "I'll see who they pair me with."

And then she could run if it turned out poorly.

She finished ensuring Kori couldn't breathe and pulled her scrub shirt over her head. She caught a glimpse of herself in the mirror and suddenly didn't need the corset. She couldn't breathe either.

What would she look like in a couple of weeks? Maybe look wasn't the right word. Feel. How would she feel? About herself. About her sexuality. About her future. Would she even want to come back to Sanctum?

"Hey?"

She shook off the emotion. She couldn't do that here and now. Nope. When she played, when whatever Dom they selected for her slapped her ass silly, then she could let herself cry. "Sorry, I spaced for a moment."

Kori stared at her as though trying to figure out how to handle the situation. "Are you sure you're okay? I heard you're talking to Jared again. He's making that documentary. I was surprised you were willing to discuss that time on camera."

"Because I'm so shy and retiring?" Those were not words she would use to describe herself. She was the woman who dressed up for pretty much everything. Dinner date? Sarah Stevens showed up in full-on pinup mode, complete with perfectly done hair and five-inch stilettos. If you came by her place for brunch, you would find her in a peignoir set with kitten heels, like she woke up in a Doris Day film. "Come on. I've been waiting for this my whole life. I've already picked out my wardrobe and the makeup."

Because in some ways it would be her armor.

"No, because you don't like to talk about it at all."

She sighed. "Just because I didn't want to sit on the shrink couch doesn't mean I'm unwilling to talk. I think it might be good for me to get it all out."

A purge of her system and then a complete reboot. Then she would have to figure out what to do with the rest of her life.

"He's totally worried about drones," Serena was complaining. "Like Ian could have put tiny drones in the flowers and they'll attack the office soon. I think it was just flowers. I think Ian was trying to be nice since it's been six months since they moved in."

"Or Ian's being a total ass," Eve replied.

Yeah, it was probably the latter. Sarah pulled out her clothes for the night. Ruby corset, check. Tiny thong, check. Sky-high heels and thigh-high hose, check and check.

What would Jared do if she showed up like that for her interview? He'd told her it would be an intimate interview, just the two of them and his camera. He was doing his own lighting.

Would he give up the icky love stuff and agree to simply do her?

"I'm glad you're talking to him," Kori said. "I think you'll find out he's changed a lot. I was surprised at how much. He's more centered than he was before. I think he knows what he wants now. He's ready to settle down. You know the last time we had dinner with him he was even talking about his biological clock. I have no idea why, but he wants kids. I tried to explain that there are lots of dogs out there, and they poop outside."

Sarah swallowed down the bile that threatened to rise. Nope. She wasn't going there. "Good for Jared. I think I'm going the same route you and Kai did. It's puppies for me. Two. Two pretty Akitas, and I already have names for them."

She shimmied out of her scrub pants. She wasn't worried that she was totally naked in front of a bunch of women who were still debating whether or not a bouquet of flowers could be an agent of evil.

Would she feel the same in two weeks' time?

A problem for another day. She eased her legs into the thong.

"Are you sure you're okay?" Kori stared at her like she knew she was missing something.

"Of course." Her bestie had been married to a shrink for way too long. "Tell me about the new guys."

"I can tell you that for the majority of the weekend, you won't know who they are unless you're really good at seeing through masks."

"Masks?" She certainly wasn't opposed. She liked the fantasy aspect.

Kori rolled her eyes because despite her job as a screenwriter, she actually wasn't so much into the fantasy thing. "The whole weekend is supposed to be done in masks and then at midnight on the last night, we take them off and reveal our identities. It's not so much fun for the married couples, but I think you'll have a blast."

"So I probably have sex with this person because I'm really horny and I can pretend I don't know this dude, and then we get to the end and I find out I slept with Boomer and my spine is suddenly as bad as Liam's." It wasn't that she thought a dude named Boomer was probably not a great lover. He probably was, and maybe he got his name because he made the ladies go boom. But still, it could be awkward.

"Just give it one night."

One night. How bad could it be? After all, she might never come back after the weekend was over.

One last wild weekend.

Chapter Three

In which rules are put into place…

Jared stared down at the mask he'd been given. It was far bigger than the one he'd worn for years on his TV show. And it wasn't green. He let his fingers brush over the ornate mask that would cover more than half his face. He'd been working on a deep tone he would have used on the film he'd gotten fired from. She shouldn't know it was him.

Was he doing the right thing? Or was he tricking her into something she didn't want?

But she'd been talking to him again. That first conversation, they'd ended up talking for hours. Nothing consequential. They'd talked about her day. He'd talked about the fact that he'd hiked the Solstice Canyon and how beautiful it was. It hadn't been deep, but it had felt like a fresh start.

It had been like that for almost two months. They'd gotten close. They'd talked almost every day.

Then nothing except professionalism from her.

He couldn't shake the thought that she was in trouble and she was hiding something. He couldn't live with himself if he didn't try.

"I don't know about this mask stuff," a deep voice said. "How does it even stay on? And honestly, my face is kind of my moneymaker when it comes to the ladies."

He turned slightly and two men were at lockers at the end of the row. Two men who looked exactly alike. He knew one of them. Michael

Malone worked at McKay-Taggart. But he wasn't sure which one Michael was because they were absolutely identical.

The one not holding the mask sighed as though they'd been over this a hundred times. "This is going to force the sub to get to know you and not just fall at your feet because you're too pretty for words. And if you don't want to play, there's the door, buddy. Feel free to walk right out. If you decide to stay, you have to follow the rules. Don't embarrass me."

The huffy twin—who was definitely Michael—stalked away and he was left staring at a man with a completely familiar look on his face. Jared knew the look because he'd seen it in the mirror about a thousand times. "Brother trouble?"

The dark-haired man with emerald green eyes sighed and put the mask down. He was already in a set of leathers, his broad chest covered in a vest. "Yeah. I thought this could be something we could do together. How stupid is that? Brotherly activities should include golf or watching baseball. When we were growing up, we rode horses together. Now if I want to spend time with my brother, I have to spank ladies."

He knew this well. "I got started in the lifestyle because my brother was involved, too. How do you actually feel about D/s? If you're not invested, you might think about not going forward. The subs here are invested in this, even if it's only for play."

"I wasn't saying I didn't take it seriously. If anything, my brother doesn't take *me* seriously."

He knew how that went, too. "You younger or older?"

Not that he supposed it meant much with twins.

"I'm two minutes older than he is."

"I'm a couple of years younger than mine and he definitely doesn't take me seriously. Well, he does now, I guess. What I'm saying is we're better now. Closer now. I didn't know Michael had a twin." He'd met Michael Malone back when he'd been doing research for the movie he hadn't made. It was sad that he could think of more projects he hadn't done than ones he had to look forward to.

The man held out of a hand. "JT Malone."

"Jared Ferguson." He probably should have called himself Master J since he intended to go by the name for the next three days, but somehow he didn't want to be anyone but himself right now. It was odd since he'd spent so much time running away from Jared John Ferguson, the boy who'd spent most of his life fucking everything up. It was funny how his most horrific fuckup had finally led him back to his family.

"Ferguson? Like Kai?" JT asked.

Jared chuckled at the irony. "Kai's my brother."

"Well, it's good to know I'm not alone." JT leaned against the locker. "I'm wondering if I should even be here at all. I do like the lifestyle. There's something easy about it. Everyone puts the rules on the table, and you have to talk about what you need. The talking part sucks. But having a woman tell me flat out what she needs and wants, that is refreshing."

"If you like the lifestyle, then stay. You never know. You might find that bond you need with your brother. I did. I learned more about my brother by figuring out D/s than I ever would if I'd stayed in the vanilla world."

A wistful smile crossed his face. "I used to think I knew everything there was to know about my brother. Maybe it's time I gave him some space. When we got out of college, I thought we would help our father run the family business. He went into the Navy. He didn't tell me until the night before he left for Great Lakes."

They had a lot in common. "Mine went Army. Our mom had just passed away and he decided that would be the best way to take care of me. He left me with an aunt and sent back money. I would have done just about anything to have had my brother instead of the money. But we're good now. He didn't do it to hurt me, though I do think there was a part of him that wanted out of the situation."

"I'm pretty sure Michael went into the Navy to get away from me or to get out from under the big old umbrella that came with our name. Our family runs a large oil company. It can be a lot of pressure. I always wanted it. He never did. Now I would give anything to feel like I had a brother at all." He sighed and stood up, reaching for the mask. "I think I'll give him some time. But that doesn't mean I can't play. I was joking about the mask. The truth is I'm a little intrigued at the idea of what a woman would think of me if she didn't see this gorgeous face of mine or know what my name is. Maybe I'll give baby brother a wide berth and start doing this just for me."

Jared had made that decision a long time ago. "I think that's a good idea. Let's go and get the lowdown on how this is supposed to work. You can hang with me. I think you'll be surprised what happens when you start ignoring your brother. Trust me. I know how to manipulate a hardass."

"No manipulation." Big Tag stepped out from behind the row of lockers. He was a massive slab of muscle and looked like he ate nails for breakfast. Jared still mourned the fact that he hadn't been the one to play Pierce Craig, the character based on Taggart. "No manipulating the other Doms. It's not manly."

"It's also not manipulation if they don't know we're doing it." At least that was how he'd always seen it. "It's just one dude doing something that might or might not make another dude do something else."

"I don't think that's going to work," JT whispered, shaking his head.

Ah, but he didn't understand Pierce Craig, and therefore Ian Taggart. At the heart of that big kickass hero lay the soul of a man who loved to have the world entertain him.

Tag's lips quirked up. "I like that. We'll use that on Kai if he figures out how you got him to do your documentary. Yeah, I know exactly what you did. That was a brilliant move, man. Kai came in all upset that someone named Kenny Asswipe—odd name for a shrink—might be on his way and we needed to keep him out of Dallas. He was serious about that. But then I checked and this guy is not on his way to Dallas. He knew nothing about the documentary. So I think you did that thing."

Jared couldn't help but grin. "I said a thing. He did a thing. I can't help it if the thing I said made him do the thing he did."

Tag pointed his way. "I like you, Johns, but the last season of *Dart* sucked."

He couldn't win them all. "Yes, it did."

"Do better next time. I liked the dart stuff," Tag said. "So you two are going to have a beautiful bromance in an attempt to make both your brothers jealous? It feels like a modern rom com. Are you going to do a makeover sequence because my sister-in-law Erin promises me she's got a soundtrack for that. My youngest brother is very much into manovers. First he talks to whatever sad-sack dude he's managed to attract, and before you know it they're crying and eating mint chocolate chip ice cream and talking about how they can be complete without a woman, and then what? Five minutes later they're trying on clothes. Oh, they'll say it's to make themselves feel better, but all those clothes show off their abs."

Yeah, he'd missed his chance to play that asshole. It hurt inside. The dumbass who'd gotten the role after he'd dropped out had made the character far too serious. "I think we'll make it through without the soundtrack or the manover. I'm perfectly comfortable with my manliness. And I'm looking for a friend. I would not hate having a cool group of guys to hang with. My best friend recently got married, and now he's focused on his wife, so I need a wingman. I figure these guys are one hundred percent murder free, right? I'm playing it safe this time."

Taggart's face lit with an unholy grin. "Oh, these are old-school deviants, but I assure you no one is a serial killer." He stopped and thought about it. "I don't think Erin can be considered a serial. They have a type, and Erin just kills assholes for fun. She doesn't discriminate. Dark hair, light hair, any nationality. Man, woman, that girl does not care. If you're an asshole and she can get away with it, she's taking the shot. Definitely not a serial. I think you're safe. Now come on and let's get the rules out of the way. I've got crazy shit to do tonight. And if you hear someone scream, it's only Adam. Don't worry about it. And you don't need the masks tonight. Those are for tomorrow. Tonight your identities are safe without the douchey costume thing. You're welcome. And I expect you to play on Friday."

He kind of thought that had been a given. Unless Tag thought he wouldn't make it to Friday. "I can't play Saturday if I don't play Friday. I definitely wouldn't miss the capture fantasy night. It's kind of my big reveal."

And then he would know if it could work between him and Sarah.

Tag shook his head. "I'm not talking about that. The throwdown is this weekend. It's the annual football game between Sanctum and The Club."

Jared wasn't exactly sure what was going on.

Big Tag stared at him with an air of expectation. "Come on. Please say it. This is my favorite part of any conversation."

Okay. He could say what he was thinking. "I thought Sanctum was the club."

"Sanctum is a club. The best club," Big Tag shot back.

Jared was still not understanding. "So we're playing football against ourselves?"

JT shook his head as though this made some sense to him. "No, we're playing against The Club."

"Which club?"

Tag grinned like this was what he lived for. "The Club."

Yes, he was definitely caught in Tag's game. "I feel like I am missing something. So there's a club called The Club?"

"Exactly, and it's full of old rich dudes who think they can play football but they can't because they're old and rich and soft," Tag pointed out. "And they're not creative with names. We have to beat them or I'll spend a year listening to Julian Lodge's snide remarks about how my guys are pudgy and slow."

"And if you win?"

Tag shrugged. "Oh, I'll call his guys pudgy and slow no matter who wins. Pretty much Lodge will too."

"So you play this game and nothing actually changes if you win?" Jared asked.

"Exactly, and I expect you to play for Sanctum. Lodge won't see it coming. I'll bench Li since half the time he tries to kick the ball when he's supposed to run with it. I blame Europe. You're in, too, Malone. I can't let Simon play either because he's a terrible athlete and also because of Europe."

Tag could be a mystery. "I think I'm safe playing a little flag football."

Tag reached out and gave his shoulder a friendly pat. "Yeah. Flag football. You keep believing that one, buddy. See you out there."

Tag strode away.

"Should I be worried?" He probably should be worried.

Jared's new friend turned his way. "I don't know. Should I be worried? Serial killer?"

Jared shrugged. "The documentary comes out next year. It'll tell you everything you need to know. That part of my life is over, but I think we should stay away from the Erin chick. Let's get this party started."

* * * *

"So we're going to meet our Doms for the weekend, but it's completely dark and we can't see them and they can't see us? And we're feeding each other a meal. In the dark?" Sarah asked, wondering how this was going to work. She gave herself one last glance in the mirror.

Charlotte Taggart nodded enthusiastically. "Yes. It's a way to get to know your play partner without any expectations. We've fitted the room with chaise lounges you'll share. You can sit apart or cuddle together.

The food is finger food and not terrifically messy. I've made sure everyone has a glass of wine or cocktail of their choice. It's going to be fun."

It didn't sound like fun. "Why am I in the corset then? If he can't see me, why didn't I stay in my scrubs?"

"You could if you want him to reach out and feel polyester," Charlotte replied.

She had a point. "My scrubs are made of organic cotton, but still not sexy. Continue."

Kori's elbow dug into her side.

She ignored her. It wasn't the first time she'd interrupted the queen to ask a question. It wouldn't be the last. It never seemed to bother Charlotte. For an alpha female, she didn't mind a few questions.

"I want every one of you to take this time to get to know the Dom who's been selected for you," Charlotte continued. "For our three nights, you will call your partner Sir and he will use a pet name of your choosing. We want you to get to know each other, to have fun with each other, and take this wherever you would like for it to go. You'll spend time with him tonight. Tomorrow you get to make the choice if you want to continue. I'll explain all of that before tomorrow evening's party. The Dom makes the choice on the final night, and then you're free to continue the relationship if you like."

"What will the couples be doing while the unattacheds are praying we're not eating anything we're allergic to?" Sarah asked. "Or that we hate a lot."

Charlotte smiled. "Well, some of us get to watch."

"Perv," Eve said with a grin. "Some of us will be setting up for the party we'll have afterward, where it will be a regular Thursday night and we have scenes going."

"That's why Tag wanted my spare night vision goggles," Erin Taggart said. She was a lovely redhead wearing a pair of leather boy shorts and a matching corset. Her hair was piled on top of her head giving her elegant lines. Sarah had always wanted to get Erin in her makeup chair. Not because she wasn't already gorgeous, but because she had such striking features they would be fun to play with.

She really should have been a makeup artist. If only it paid as well as saving lives.

"You have a spare set of night vision goggles?" Serena Dean-Miles asked.

Erin shrugged. "Doesn't everyone?"

Apparently Big Tag didn't, or maybe he'd borrowed for a friend. "So we have creepers?"

Charlotte grinned. "Of course. Where would the fun be without them? Also, before we get started, is everyone ready for the annual throwdown?"

It was one of the best times of the year. She got to sit on a picnic blanket outrageously overdressed for the occasion and watch as hot guys pretended like they could play football. And she would bring wine and cheese. Kori would bring a bunch of dogs who would try to eat her cheese, but it was okay because they were awfully cute. There was only one problem this year. She groaned. "I know I usually bring snacks, but I might have to send them with Kori. I promised Jared Johns I would work on his documentary this weekend."

Because she wouldn't be able to next weekend. God, she would rather think about hot guys who pretended they could play football.

Charlotte shook her head. "Not happening. I have it on good authority Ian views Jared's arrival in time for the annual game as a sign from heaven that we're going to win this year. I'm going to warn you though. He's going to bench Liam and Si because of, well, the fact that they spend a lot of time trying to explain that it's not real football. Sorry Avery and Chels."

Avery stood next to Charlotte's sister Chelsea, who was married to Simon Weston. "No problem. He's still not over the Boomer incident."

Chelsea frowned at her sister. "You know Simon thinks he's an athlete. How do I explain that he's getting shoved aside for some actor?"

"Jared is an actual athlete." The words came out of Sarah's mouth before she could call them back. Everyone turned and stared at her. Yep, she should have kept her mouth shut. "He was on *American Ninja Warrior* and everything. He made it through the whole course."

She'd only watched it about three hundred times. It wasn't her fault manly muscles did something for her.

So did his sweetness. She couldn't help but remember how close she'd come to giving in and going to Malibu to see him. She'd known he would ask her when they'd started talking on the phone again. She'd fallen into his smooth tones and funny stories and the way he could make her feel like she was the only woman in the world when he focused on her. When they were talking, he wasn't playing around on his computer or working out. He was talking to her and had attention for nothing else. She never had to say something twice to Jared.

Kori had a hand on her hip. "You sound like you care."

"I do. About ninja things." She wasn't about to talk about how much she cared about Jared John Ferguson. Because she couldn't. Because he would want far more than she could ever give him now. "I'm only saying that he probably plays football well. Maybe Simon could be a cheerleader."

The big Brit would look good jumping up and down.

Chelsea's lips curled in a grin. "I'll pass that on. And I want a lot of cheese. Now that I'm not throwing up constantly I want to eat. A lot. Who's bringing the sweets?"

"Macon and Ally." Charlotte gave her sister an encouraging nod. "And Avery has promised to bring the Icy Hot."

"I went to Costco," Avery admitted. "It's big in our house after Fight Club."

The other women continued to talk but Kori took her by the elbow and led her over to the side of the locker room.

"Why are you doing this when Jared is in town?" Kori asked, her voice low. "You know you want to see him."

"I am seeing him." She was going to get in trouble because she hadn't told Kori much of anything lately. It was probably best to tell her this so she didn't have to reveal anything more. "I'm doing the interview for the documentary."

"That's not seeing him. Not really. That's a work thing, though you should know he's probably going to try to talk to you about more than the interview."

"Then I'll have to shut him down." She knew he would use this time to try to talk to her about their friendship, but she hadn't been able to refuse one last chance to see him. He would move on eventually. He was too amazing and he wanted a family so much. Some woman would snap him up, and she would likely be a gorgeous actress with a fabulous career. "I just want to find some closure. I'm sure Kai would think it was good for me if I were to ever talk about feelings stuff with him. Which I will not."

Kori stared at her for a moment. "He would say it's a good thing. You do need closure. I'm supposed to do an interview, too. It's going to be hard to relive the day, but I think Jared needs this."

She glanced back to where Charlotte was starting to lead the subs toward the "dark room" as she'd called it.

She stared at the door in front of her. It was one of the main rooms in the dungeon, one that normally was reserved for suspension play. She knew the room well since nothing made her happier than being held in ropes like a work of art for all to look at.

She might be an exhibitionist.

That room was not about exhibitionism this evening.

"And I think *I* need *this*."

Kori reached out and squeezed her hand. "I wish you would talk to me. I know something's going on."

Sarah had to force back tears. She wasn't doing this. It was precisely why she hadn't told her bestie. "I'm not ready to talk about it, but you should know I'm handling it. I'm going to be fine."

It was blatantly obvious her bestie didn't want to let it drop, but she sighed. "All right. I'm going to help Kai set up a hard point. You have fun. I want to hear everything about it when you're done."

She nodded and let go of Kori's hand. It was time to see if she could make a connection.

Chapter Four

In which connections are made and chocolate is had...

It was dark. Super dark. She was sure one of the guys could compare this darkness to a cave they'd explored or a moonless night in the forest, but she wasn't much of a camper. The Four Seasons always had a light she could turn on.

"I suppose if one of us breaks a leg walking around in the dark, I'm going to have to set it," she muttered as she took another step.

"I've got night vision on," Adam Miles said. He was her "escort" basically meaning it was his job to ensure she made it to the Dom without falling all over herself. "It's okay. I'm going to get you to your station and make sure you're comfortable. Then you should know there are a couple of us staying behind to monitor the situation and ensure your safety."

"Or to watch to see if any of us go for it and fuck in the dark." She knew what they were really here for.

"Or that," Adam allowed. "All right. You're here and this is your Sir. Sir, your submissive for the night wishes to be called Princess."

A big hand covered her own, an immediate heat flashing through her system. That hand was callused and rough, the hand of a man who worked, and not sitting at a typewriter. "Hello, Princess."

That voice. Deep and strong, with a hint of Western accent. He sounded almost like...that was just where her mind was going tonight. Straight to Jared, but he didn't have a hint of an accent and he always sounded so happy. Like nothing could bring him down ever. There was gravity to this man's voice.

"Hello, Sir."

He held her hand in his and covered it with his other, enveloping her in his warmth. Without being able to see him, she would be forced to focus on his touch and the sound of his voice. She wasn't thinking about whether he was handsome or plain. She was thinking about how good his hand felt holding hers, how soothing his voice was.

"I'm going to help you sit down now. There's a chaise lounge half a foot to your right. I'll help you sit, and then I'm going to take the space to your left. In front of the chaise is a small table and there's another to the left side that I will feed you from."

He was going to feed her. "All right."

At some point Adam must have moved away because all she could sense was Sir. "Can we wait a moment? Could I touch you? I just want to get a feel for how tall you are."

"Only if I can touch you as well."

That sent a delicious shiver through her. "Yes."

"Give me your other hand." He kept one in his left palm and she placed the other on top of his free hand.

He flipped it over and seemed to take a moment, his thumbs running over her palms, studying her hands as though he could memorize them. He threaded their fingers together, sliding them along until they felt like puzzle pieces that had gently found their place.

"You're not a regular here." She'd been told he wouldn't be, but somehow she didn't think he was from The Club either.

He brought her right hand up and placed it on his chest. His skin was warm, a light dusting of chest hair tickling against her palm. "No. I'm not from Dallas. I live out on the West Coast. I have a couple of friends who live here. You're from Texas?"

She knew there were other people around them. There were twenty subs and Doms participating, and probably another ten watching whether for safety or prurient pleasure. Big Tag and his wife were probably doing pervy things somewhere in this room, but all she could hear was the deep timbre of his voice. "Yes. I've lived here most of my life. I've moved around the metroplex, but I've stayed in North Texas."

She ran her hands slowly over his chest and up to broad shoulders. She could feel the edges of his leather vest, soft against her skin. The leather was buttery and likely worn.

His fingertips brushed over her, finding the line of her neck like he was exploring each curve and valley. "You don't have an accent. I would expect Texas girls to have a twang."

She chuckled, covering the shiver his touch was sending through her. "Not in the big cities. Dallas is very international. It's full of people who came from other places, and it tends to affect our accents. I grew up surrounded by kids who were from Michigan and California and New York. It's a big old melting pot."

"I like that." The words were said with a chuckle that seemed to caress her skin. "Is your hair up?"

"You can take it down if you like, Sir. It's held up by a single pin." She'd piled it on her head, pulling down some tendrils to frame her face before she'd understood no one was really looking at her tonight. Not until the after party.

Would she be able to tell who her Sir was? Would she look out over the crowded dungeon and know his broad shoulders and muscular chest? He had to be six two or three since she was forced to reach up to smooth her hands over his shoulders, loving the moment she passed the soft leather to find his skin.

She forced herself to breathe as he gently framed her face with his big hands and then brushed them up and over her hair until he found the antique hair pin that held her loose bun in place.

"Does this double as a weapon?"

She smiled as she explored the warm flesh of his neck. He was incredibly fit, but lean, too. His neck wasn't massive like some steroided-out gym maniac. "No, Sir. It was a gift from my grandmother meant only to look pretty."

"I have to ask given where we are. Some of the women are deadly."

He wasn't wrong about that. The Sanctum crowd had a whole lot of ex-military or former/current law enforcement. "I'm a 'save lives' kind of girl. No spy stuff for me. Well, except when it comes to gossip, and then I will spy like James Bond."

He gently pulled the pin from her bun and it tumbled free, falling around her shoulders and down past her breasts. He sighed as he threaded his fingers through her hair, running them along her scalp and down until he brushed the tops of her breasts. "Gossip girl?"

That did sound kind of bad. She should explain. It was hard to find words when her nipples had tightened to almost the point of pain. Luckily, she liked erotic pain. A lot. "Only in a good way. I'll be honest, one of the reasons I like Sanctum is the lack of nastiness. Since Queen

Charlotte banished a bunch of subs for bad behavior, we don't have a ton of mean girls. Well, we have Maia, but only when Big Tag needs her to manipulate the legal and political systems to do his will. That happens surprisingly more than you would think it does."

"She's the ADA?"

"She won the DA's race a couple of months ago, so I expect she'll be around a lot. She's mean, but like to everyone, so it's hard to take it personally."

"She's mean to you?" The question came out hard, and she was pretty sure if she could have seen his eyes, they would have narrowed.

She'd expected an alpha male. Sanctum was full of them, and the Doms liked to take care of subs. She couldn't take that personally either. "Not really. She's got a sharp tongue and she was born without a single fuck to give. I can handle myself. But like I was saying one of the reasons I love it here is the lack of nastiness, so when it comes to gossip, it's usually stuff like friends doing silly things. Like Jesse Murdoch and Simon Weston having a secret bet on who can stay on the hamster wheel the longest."

The hamster wheel was a giant…well, hamster wheel. It was in the largest of the dungeons in the club and for the most part was used to "punish" subs by making them light the sucker up. The faster the sub ran the more colors they lit up. If she was in any way interested in running, it would have been fun.

She was not.

"Who won?"

"We all did because they thought they could come in after hours and have their runoff in private, but my friend Vince overheard them in the locker room and we snuck back in. There's apparently a trick to running on a circular track that neither one of them got. The good news was we had a laugh and I got to snap Jesse's shoulder back into place."

His hand was in her hair as though he couldn't quite stop touching it. "And what was your punishment? You snuck in and watched two Doms who were looking for privacy. There should have been punishment."

Every word was deep and dark, honey rich and ripe with promise. What would this man's punishment be like? "Did you forget the whole snapping his shoulder back into place part?"

"I did not. I also didn't forget the disrespect part."

"Vince did have to spend three days crawling around. Mistress

Jackie is his Domme and she takes that stuff seriously. Master Kai put Kori in some pretty nasty bondage for a whole evening. He carted her around like a piece of luggage and she wasn't allowed to speak. She really hates the ball gag."

"And what happened to you?" Sir asked.

"I was the chick who saved Master Jesse's ability to throw a baseball."

His hand fisted in her hair sending the most delicious thrill down her spine as he tugged to just the right side of pain. "No one punished you?"

"It's not that kind of club. I don't have a Dom and Big Tag is surprisingly indulgent if he likes a person."

He pressed up and forced her to her toes. Her breath hitched as she felt his warmth close to her ears. "Poor sub. You should know if you decide to dance for me tomorrow night, I would have punished you. I would have put you over my knee and spanked your ass silly. I would have forced you to stay at my side and serve my every need, and many of those needs would have been sexual. I would have kept you naked and desperate for my affection."

Charlotte was totally right to have done this because she didn't care what he looked like. All that mattered was how he made her feel and that was desired and achy and super, super horny.

"I'll keep that in mind, Sir." She couldn't help the way her breath came out in little puffs.

Yes, she could spend the weekend with this man. He wouldn't be here for long. He would stay for the weekend and maybe come back from time to time since he had friends here, but she wouldn't get invested in him. She would be smart and safe.

"Let's sit for a while," he whispered. "I want to talk to you. I want to get to know you, Princess. I want to know if the name you've picked for yourself is perfect or perfectly ironic because I think you might be a horrible, wicked little brat."

"Do you like brats?" She'd known some Doms who didn't, who wanted a perfectly obedient sub. They didn't come to Sanctum. Sanctum was what she liked to call sugar kink. It was for play and no one took it too seriously. Brattiness was often seen as entertainment.

"I'm fucking crazy about a truly luscious brat," he admitted. "Nothing in the world can make me happier than getting a brat to smile my way. And to cry a little, but only if she needs it."

She spoke his language. He liked to play but wasn't afraid of a challenge. It was exactly the type of Dom she adored.

Years she'd waited, wondering if one of the members in charge of pairing up people would find her a dream Dom. She was the sub who got to break in the baby Doms because they knew she was fun and kind and wouldn't get serious about anyone.

She couldn't get serious about this guy. Couldn't. But she could play with him. She could pretend. "I know you can't see me right now, but I'm smiling at you, Sir."

She felt his hands soften in her hair and something warm brushed her eye.

He pulled away and chuckled. "Sorry. I don't think that was your forehead. It was supposed to be your forehead."

It was good to know he wasn't perfect. "It's okay. I think I'm rubbing your ear right now."

"Hey, it's totally working for me." He went quiet for a moment. "Sit with me."

"I'd like that."

* * * *

Jared settled himself on the couch, happy he hadn't fallen on his ass. The dark thing was interesting but it was also fraught with peril. He'd done so well. He'd managed to get her hair down, to touch her and sink his hands into all that soft stuff. He'd always been fascinated by her hair. There was so much of it. She put it up most of the time, whether it was in a messy bun or one of her elaborate updos. He wanted her to let it down for him, had fantasized about what that hair would feel like when she draped herself around him after he'd made her scream.

Why had he fucking waited? When he'd met her, he'd wanted her. Right from the start. He'd taken one look at her curvy pinup girl figure and stunning face and known he wanted to get her in bed. Then he'd spent time with her and realized she was far more than a gorgeous face and banging body. Sarah was funny, weird in the best way. She saw the world differently and it was a world he wanted to live in.

By then he'd fucked things up entirely, and now he had to do anything he could to make it right.

Or he was tricking her and it would bite him in the ass. He had to take the chance. He had to get inside her head and figure out what the problem was—because he was one hundred percent sure there was a problem. Sarah wasn't the type of woman who ghosted a man.

He held her hand in his. "I would love it if you would sit on my lap. It will make things so much easier, but if you're not comfortable with me yet, I understand and we can each have our own space."

She was quiet for a moment but then her hand squeezed his. "I'd like that, Sir. Can I be honest with you?"

"I would greatly prefer it if you were." *Even though I'm not being honest with you since I know damn well who you are.*

"I'd like to do these sessions with you. I might even like to move it to a physical level at some point, but I'm not interested in anything serious right now."

He hated the hollow sound in her tone. Maybe if the lights had been on and he'd been distracted by her face, he wouldn't have caught that tiny hitch in her breath that let him know she was emotional. "We don't have to decide anything right now. We're just two people getting to know each other in the dark. Can we take it one night at a time?"

Her hand came out of his. "I need you to know this will end when the weekend does."

"May I ask why?"

She was silent for a moment and he could hear the low murmur of people around them, though he couldn't make out the actual words. It was the first real reminder that they were not alone.

"I'm not interested in a relationship right now."

"What's your definition of a relationship?" he asked. "Are you telling me after this weekend no matter how compatible we seem to be, you won't be interested in playing with me again?"

"You'll be gone, right?"

Was this her way of protecting herself? "I don't live in Dallas, but like I said, I have friends here. I miss them. I think I want to come here and see them more often, but no I won't be around all the time." He meant to take her with him when he left.

"So you'll come back to Sanctum."

He liked the hope he heard in her voice. "Yes, I absolutely will come back to Sanctum. I don't have a sub. When I come back, I'll want someone to play with. Princess, this is three days. I don't think we'll figure anything out in three days. Can we go with the flow? Enjoy this long weekend and then if we both would like to later on, we can play again."

It might be a longer game than he'd planned on, but he could improvise. He needed his Jared side to get her talking in person. Sir could be the fantasy Dom. One would work on her body and the other her soul. What he wasn't willing to do was let her go.

"I think I can do that." Her hand bumped into his and he tugged her down.

It was awkward at first, but she managed to set herself on his lap. She wriggled against him, trying to find a comfortable position. Or being a mega brat who wanted to see if she could make him as uncomfortable as possible since his dick had already responded to having her hands on his skin. He'd gotten aroused at her running her palms across his chest. He was hard as hell as her lush backside seemed to need to rub against every inch of him she could touch.

"Sorry, Sir."

There it was, that husky tone that let him know she'd moved from princess to brat. Or maybe she was always there—his brat princess. He wound his arm around her back, supporting her. Her arm came up around his neck and he breathed her in. He craved her scent. Like daisies and sunshine. It took everything he had not to run his nose along her neck and take that smell into his lungs.

"Don't apologize. I enjoy it. I might be a Dom, but every man's a masochist when it comes to this." God knew he was. He would take her teasing him as long as it meant she was here.

"Are you ready for the first course?" a deep voice to his right asked.

Sarah squealed and if he hadn't been quick, she would have ended up on the floor. Her arms clutched him and she cuddled close.

He did the same, liking the darkness more and more. "It's just our helper. Didn't Charlotte tell you we would have a person who can see helping us if we need it? He's going to make sure I don't screw up the courses."

"I assure you she wasn't listening," the man to his right replied with a chuckle. "She's known for following the shiny objects of this world. I think this whole exercise might have been tailored to force her to focus."

"I can't help it if I enjoy the beautiful things of life," she protested. "And that's the last time I save your shoulder blade, Master Jesse."

Ah, so now he knew who his helper was. Jesse Murdoch. He'd met the man but hadn't gotten close to him.

"Somehow I doubt that," Murdoch replied, his tone low and

soothing. "Princess here is known for being incredibly kind, though I do believe she could use someone willing to take responsibility for her. She can be a heinous brat."

"I only vaguely resemble that remark," Sarah shot back but she'd settled in again.

"For the next three nights, I'm responsible for you," Jared replied. "At least while we're playing I am."

"I would like to…" she began.

He knew exactly where she was going. It was not the first time he'd heard this lecture. "You are a strong, individual female who can take care of herself in and out of the club, but we're playing and we're going to play like I'm responsible for you, like I'm here to do nothing more than care for you, ensure you're safe. I'm going to pretend, while we're in this club, like my whole job is to make you happy. Can you play with me like that?"

"Meow." She laid her head against his chest.

"That means she agrees," Murdoch explained. "She's got some quirks, that one."

"I resemble that, too," she whispered.

He thought her quirks were utterly adorable. And their views of D/s had always seemed to align perfectly. They played in the club. They played when they agreed to it, but in real life, they were comfortable with more blurry lines when it came to their roles in the relationship. He didn't want to have to hide himself from her. He wanted her to share his sorrow and his pain, his life in all its good and bad. She was strong enough. "Are you hungry?"

"It depends."

On what he was going to feed her. "You have to take this part on faith."

"I'm ready, Sir."

"The plate is to your right," Murdoch explained. "When you're done with the first course, I'll set out the second, and then the third. I'll be close if you need me, but I'm going to be quiet now unless you need something else."

"You're going to be watching because you're a pervy perv," Sarah said, her sass coming out.

Murdoch laughed. "Probably. So do something interesting."

That was not going to fly tonight. This was a formal session. The rules had been laid out. "Master Jesse, I apologize for my brat's impoliteness."

"She was just joking. It's what we do," Jesse replied.

"Not while I'm her Dom and we're in a very formal setting." He wasn't about to let her treat this like a damn joke.

"I didn't mean anything," Sarah said quietly.

"Then you can apologize to the man helping us and then you can flip yourself over my lap and we can get the punishment out of the way."

She went completely still. "You're going to spank me?"

Was this how she got through life? Because she was soft and sweet and funny and everyone let her slide? He knew the plan well and knew that while it looked good on the surface, it had left him feeling alone, like no one cared enough to fight with him. Yes, he understood that life well. "You don't need to sound so surprised. You've been in the lifestyle for a long time if you were invited to this party. I was told there were no newbies here. Was I misinformed? Are you a tourist?"

Oh, that got her to sit up straight. "I've been in the lifestyle for years, Sir. I've taken a spanking about a thousand times."

"Excellent, then you know how to assume the position and how to handle this with grace. And before you try to get out of this by saying you didn't know it was wrong to be impolite in a formal setting, it won't fly with me. You've already told me you're not interested in a relationship outside the club. You only want a brief D/s relationship. Well, this is what it looks like. Take the spanking and we can get back to the part where I indulge you on every level."

"I have to think about it." She gave him mere seconds before she spoke again. "Are you a hardass Dom?"

She didn't need that, but she did need one who called her on her shit in the proper setting. She needed one who made her take this seriously from time to time. "No. I'm a Dom who thinks he knows what you need. I think everyone else gets the treats, don't they? Those happy D/s couples, they get to play in a way we don't. A Dom with a sub gets to spank her pretty ass because it belongs to him. A sub with a Dom never knows when he's going to spank her so she can't let her guard down. She has to know he's always watching her, waiting to see if he can steal a chance to put his hands on her."

"They do get all the treats."

She slid off his lap and he knew he had her.

At least for now.

Chapter Five

In which an ass is smacked and our hero wishes the darkness could last forever...

Treats. What he'd said was true. She could be as bratty as she liked and the most she got was Big Tag threatening to put her on double nursery duty. No one ever dropped everything he was doing and demanded she lie over his lap for some much needed discipline.

It had been a long time since she'd had a Dom of her own, and even then Tommy had been more about getting through it so he could have sex. He hadn't been a bad guy. He just hadn't been the right one for her.

She'd always thought in the back of her head that she would have that moment, the one where she looked across the crowded dungeon and she just knew. One day her Dom would come and he would sweep her off her feet and he wouldn't make her fall madly in love with him and then leave without saying good-bye or even giving her more than a single kiss.

She bit back a groan because she wasn't going to think about Jared tonight. Not when she had a Dom saying the right things, one who wouldn't break her heart if he left because she wasn't going to get too involved.

A Dom who knew what he was talking about. Spankings were treats with the right Dom. With the right Dom she would have to walk into the dungeon and wonder if he was watching because he would always be looking for a reason to smack her ass silly and then make her do nasty things to make up for her bad behavior.

She probably had paternal issues, but she didn't care. She knew what she wanted and right now it was to see how well Sir could take care of her.

Maybe he would be terrible at spanking. He could hit too hard or not hard enough. He could have terrible rhythm. It was dark. He could miss and end up hitting Jesse or the food. Then she wouldn't have to be so damn curious about him.

There was soft carpet under her knees. She knew this part of the dungeon well. The floor was stained concrete, but someone had known more than one set of knees would likely hit the ground tonight. She reached up and felt the leather of Sir's pants. It was easier than she'd thought it would be to position herself over his lap.

She immediately had to draw in a hard breath because Sir's hand did not have trouble in the dark. He might have struggled to find her forehead with his lips, but his hand seemed magnetized to her ass cheeks. He caressed her and she could feel he hadn't lost any steam.

She didn't need to see his dick to know how long and hard it could get.

"It's a count of thirty," he said, his voice deep and rich. "You can stop me at any time. All you have to do is say your safe word. What is it?"

"I use red because sometimes when I'm involved I forget the cutesy ones."

"Red it is, then."

The smack of his hand on her ass sounded like thunder in the quiet of the space. Pain flared through her, making her eyes water, but even as the fire spiked she already knew this was going to be perfect.

The room seemed to have gone silent, the sound of her flesh being slapped echoing through. They were listening, every one of them wondering which brat had managed to piss off her brand-new Dom so quickly. Pervs. She loved it. She would proudly tell everyone she was the one who'd taken the first spanking of the celebrations.

A treat between her and Sir.

A treat that was making tears drip from her eyes and dirty words bite on her tongue because she wasn't foolish enough to say them at this point. She wasn't sure how Sir would take her unleashing an unholy amount of fucks into their disciplinary time.

Over and over he slapped her ass, somehow never seeming to hit the same spot too many times. He was an experienced Dom, not a baby. He was probably older, maybe a gorgeous silver fox.

Oh, wouldn't that be wonderful? A man who knew who he was, who'd lived a life and wanted to find some peace with a sub he could care about, share the rest of his time with.

She could do that.

"Where are you?" his deep voice asked.

He'd only given her half of what he'd promised, but again he was proving to be a careful Dom by making sure she verbally acknowledged how she felt. He couldn't see her so verbal cues would be everything to him.

"I'm perfectly green, Sir. I'm going to admit to you that I'm a little bit of a pain slut. This isn't really punishment for me, but I'm also not such a brat that I would have misbehaved just to get this out of you." She should qualify that. "Not yet, at least."

He caressed her backside, his hand moving from bare flesh to snap at her thong. "I think we're going to get along perfectly well, Princess. Now for the rest."

Her whole body lit up with the pain he gave her—always controlled. Her words seemed to have slightly let him off his leash and she gritted her teeth against the hard smacks he delivered. She wasn't sure why this did it for her. She joked about daddy issues, but she didn't really have them. She was born kinky and she was okay with that. The pain sensitized her, awakened her senses the way gentle caresses might for another woman. There was nothing wrong with either. Sex, like love, had many, many forms. She'd been lucky enough to have found partners who'd never given her a sense of shame.

By the time he delivered the final smack, she could feel her whole body go soft and warm and languid. Her ass was sore but it wouldn't last more than an hour or so. That was disappointing, but she had the weekend to play with him. He was her personal Dom for the weekend, and she was already planning her wardrobe for tomorrow night's party.

There was no way she wasn't dancing for this guy.

"I think you should apologize to our helper." The words weren't cold. They were a warm reminder that the ritual wasn't complete.

"I'm sorry for calling you a pervy perv, Master Jesse."

In the background someone groaned. "I should have known it would be her."

Kori. Yep, her pervy perv bestie knew her voice well.

Jesse chuckled. "Not a problem. Enjoy the rest of your evening."

She gasped as Sir somehow managed to pick her up and flip her over. Oh, this man was full of muscley goodness. He'd made her feel like she didn't weigh a thing. She was settled back in his lap in a few seemingly easy moves. Her heart rate ticked up again.

"All right, Brat Princess. Let's see if we can get through the rest of the evening without more punishment," he whispered against her ear. "The next time I spank your ass, I want to see it. I think it's very likely a spectacularly glorious ass."

She wanted to see him, too, but she'd decided to embrace the whole exercise. "I look forward to it, Sir."

"Tell me how you got into the lifestyle. Here, I think this one is yours," he offered and what was probably a straw hit her nose.

She reached up and brought the straw to her lips. Pineappley perfection coated her tongue. "Yum, piña colada."

"I'm glad I got that right. Luckily your drink is cold and mine is room temperature, as a good bourbon should be." His hand caressed her leg as she took control of the drink. "Now tell me how you got into the lifestyle."

It was the question that started many a conversation between Dom and sub. "I was nineteen and I got invited to a play party by this guy on campus and I went."

He was quiet for a moment. "A boyfriend?"

"Nah, a guy in my chemistry class. I kind of knew him. He turned out to be a super jerk, but I met a whole bunch of people."

"You know that was dangerous, right?"

Thank god it was dark and he couldn't see how fast she rolled her eyes. "Yes. I know this now. At the time it felt like an adventure. Kind of like this. Luckily I haven't been murdered yet, and if you knew my history you would think that's a miracle."

He stiffened and for a moment, she worried she'd said something wrong. "Well, I'm glad you're okay. There are dangerous people out there. A sub has to be careful. A Dom has to be careful. I'm hoping you don't go to random play parties anymore."

"Big Tag would kick my ass," she admitted. "I don't need to explore that way anymore. Sanctum is safe, but I know all the Doms. I haven't made a strong connection beyond friendship with any of them. The last time I had a regular Dom was years and years ago. Now I just play but it almost never gets serious." Meaning sexual. God, it had been forever since she'd had sex. "There was a guy a while back who I thought might be interested, but it didn't work out."

"Really? Why didn't it work out?"

Because Jared Johns had been a douchebag idiot who hadn't stuck around to fight it out with her and then when she thought they might get it all together…well, she couldn't blame him for that. "Our timing was always bad. When I wanted something serious, he wasn't ready. When he did, I wasn't."

"Why weren't you ready? I mean, if you were before, what happened to make you not ready?"

A little spit had happened. "People change. I changed. So how about you? How did you decide to become a big, bad Dom?"

"I didn't have a lot of discipline growing up," he admitted. "Not that I was a bad kid, but I was the kind of kid who skated by on charm, if you know what I mean. When the world went bad, it hit me hard. I ended up in the lifestyle because someone I admired had taught himself discipline through it. There were times in my life when I wasn't in control of anything, and I learned that if I could master myself enough to take care of someone else, that could sometimes be the thing I needed to hold myself together."

So he was super strong, charming, and willing to make himself vulnerable. Too many Doms came in with "I was born to dominate, baby. I can't give up control." What they really meant was that they were selfish assholes. It was why she loved Sanctum. Big Tag tended to weed them out pretty quick. "Rough childhood?"

"Not at all. That was the point. I had a lovely childhood, though it wasn't a wealthy one. We were poor. My father wasn't around, but my older brother was. My mom…I still miss my mother."

"I do, too." The darkness allowed her to do what she wouldn't in the light. It let her allow the tears that pierced her eyes to drop onto her cheeks. "I miss her every day. My dad, too. I was a late in life baby for them. I think they'd given up on the idea. Then oops, here I come when they were both in their forties. Sometimes I think I became a nurse because I knew I would have to take care of them. And I wasn't supposed to talk about specifics. I'm sorry."

"I think those rules are going to be very hard to follow," he replied. "Telling me you're a nurse isn't something I'm going to spank you for. I find it fascinating. I haven't had a permanent partner."

"Never?" That was surprising. He seemed so comfortable with the lifestyle.

"No. I'm afraid my career took up a lot of my time. I belong to a club on the West Coast. I have several subs I play with on a regular basis, but I travel a lot for business and it didn't come together for me. I'm looking to slow down a bit, move into another phase of my career."

Was he looking to retire? "I wouldn't mind slowing down and seeing something of the world. I think that's what I'll do next. I want to take some time off from work and travel. Both of my parents are gone so I don't have anyone to take care of."

His hand stroked across her thighs. "Traveling is a good thing. I've seen a whole lot of the world, but I admit I didn't take it into my soul the way I should have. When I was younger all I could see was my own ambition. Now when I travel I like to take my time, get to understand where I am in the world. Hand me your drink. I think we're ready for the first course."

She managed to get the piña colada back in his hand and relaxed. Sir was a comfortable seat despite the muscles. He was comfortable to be around period. His easy manner coupled with the fact that he knew how to play made it all more possible that this would be the weekend she needed.

If only she could stop thinking about the one who'd gotten away. When Sir had talked about his childhood, she'd wondered about Jared's. She'd known he'd grown up rough, not without love, but with a million financial insecurities she didn't understand. His world had seemed precarious.

And it had been precarious, as his friend had proven. She could still remember how the police had come in and pulled him from her arms. Their first kiss. Their only kiss.

"Are you ready?" Sir asked.

She had to be because she couldn't go back. She couldn't be the Sarah Jared needed, and that meant moving on. Even if only for the weekend. "I am."

She breathed in the scent of what he offered her. Strawberries and cream. She loved them.

It had to be enough for now.

* * * *

"Seriously, you already spanked your sub?" JT seemed more relaxed after two hours of conversation with the woman chosen for him.

Jared glanced around the locker room. Most of the Doms had simply moved to the party going on in the largest of the dungeon spaces. He could hear the thud of music playing through the club. He'd been told there was a nice buffet since all they'd had were finger foods during the initial meeting, and there was supposed to be a couple of interesting teaching scenes.

He wouldn't be going to any of it. He couldn't risk it. No one was wearing masks tonight. They weren't supposed to mingle with the potential submissives, but there was no doubt Sarah would have questions if she saw him. Forceful questions she would likely yell at the top of her lungs.

"Princess turns out to be a sweet brat who deserved to get her backside blistered, and I meant that in a good way because she liked it." He hated hearing her talk about how she didn't have a Dom even though he was happy about it, too. It made him realize how much he'd hurt them both by walking away. His guilt had sent him running, but it had done more than that. It had left her lonely. His guilt had hurt them both.

He wanted to walk out there and see her. She looked gorgeous in fet wear, her breasts pushed up and on display. He'd felt the boning of her corset and had wanted so badly to know the color she was wearing and how it showed off her skin. Well, what he'd wanted to do was drag her mouth to his and kiss her until she couldn't think straight, and then get her on her back under him.

Instead he'd fed her and talked to her. He'd reveled in how funny she was, how much he adored the sound of her voice.

JT grinned and leaned against the lockers. "Mine likes to be called Sweetie. She seems nice. Maybe this wasn't a bad idea after all."

It was nice to hang out with a person who seemed to have no idea who he was.

Or maybe he was overestimating his own celebrity. It had been a while since *Dart* aired, since he'd had a decent role in a movie. He had a couple of projects he had supporting roles in coming out next year, but mostly now he seemed to be known for being a serial killer's best friend. Or the guy who got away with it all.

Of course it also could be that Big Tag had told everyone to pretend like they didn't know him.

He dragged his T-shirt over his head. "You liked Sweetie?"

"She seemed nice. I don't know how well it's going to work out in the long run, but hey, I'll give it a weekend," JT admitted. "I take it you liked Princess pretty well."

He was crazy in love with Princess, but he couldn't tell anyone. "She's pretty much exactly my type."

"How can you know that if you didn't see her?"

"She sat in my lap. I got a good feel for her. She's got a great body and thick, long hair." And the most beautiful eyes. He didn't need to see them to remember those. He could still see her staring at him as he'd turned and walked away. He could still see the hurt stamped on her face and the stubborn will there. He'd known in that moment that she would move on.

Except she hadn't.

The question was what had she meant about their timing always being off? He knew she'd been talking about him when she'd mentioned a man who might have been her Dom. He hadn't been ready then. She wasn't ready now. The longing had been plain in her voice. Why wasn't she ready? Because she couldn't forgive him?

"I didn't think about that," JT mused. "I should have gotten her in my lap. I'll be honest, I was just happy not to fall. The darkness stuff was a little intimidating, but it also forced me to talk to her. All in all, not a terrible night."

"There you are." Michael rounded the corner. He had his hands on his hips and stared at his brother. "I've been looking for you. I thought we were meeting up after."

JT shrugged negligently. "I don't remember saying that. I was just hanging with my friend here. Jared, you've met my brother, right? I apologize that he didn't say hello before. He was far too busy lecturing me."

Michael frowned and it was obvious he hadn't expected his brother to make friends. "I was only trying to make sure you understood the rules. Come on. There's barbecue. Sean Taggart catered this thing. It's really good. Almost better than Dad's, but don't tell him I said that."

"Our dad's an oil man. Sean's a chef. He would understand." JT gave Jared a wave. "I guess I'll see you tomorrow at the game."

Where he would come face to face with Sarah for the first time. Tonight didn't count since he couldn't see her face and she hadn't known it was him. "See you there."

Maybe he would take off his shirt. He could find a reason. She liked him without his shirt on. She would sit and watch him work out like he was putting on a show for her. He could play that angle.

But tonight, he would go back to his room at Kai's place alone. It was a penance of sorts.

"You're not coming to the party?" Kai seemed to have followed Michael into the locker room.

Sometimes a little jealousy was a good thing. Not that he was going to rub his brother's nose in it, but it looked like being friendly with JT had gotten both of their brothers to seek them out. All JT had needed was a little brother to show him how to grab attention. He was a master at it.

If only he could get Sarah's…

"I think going to the party would be a bad idea," he admitted. "Too many questions. I think she would want to know what I'm doing here and then I would have to lie to her more than I already am."

"You could walk out there and tell her you were the Dom she spent the evening with." Kai sat on the bench.

"I think that's a great way to get her to kick me to the curb." He wasn't sure he would get another chance with her. "I need to be patient."

Kai rolled his eyes. "We have different definitions of that word. It's only three days. There's not a lot of patience with that. So do you think she's going to pick you tomorrow? That's the deal. You two spend time together tonight and then tomorrow we're having a big harem party. Apparently Charlotte has a costume and she's been dying to show it off. That couple has crazy kinks, and that's saying something coming from me. I heard her talk about the shoe fairy and how she gets caught by the fairy king and is forced to do all kinds of nasty sex stuff or give up her Louboutins. Who thinks that kind of thing up?"

He could. He would love to role-play with his gorgeous pinup girl. He would buy a treasure trove of costumes for her. But role-playing wasn't his brother's thing, and Charlotte wasn't being entirely historically accurate. "I don't think concubines got to decide who they danced for."

Kai chuckled. "Worried, are you?"

He sighed and sat down beside his brother. "A little. We got along great tonight."

"Well, she does like a spanking. I think everyone was a bit shocked the new guy went right there. Of course they had no idea you know exactly what Sarah likes and how hard she likes it. You've played with her before, even if it was brief. So it went well this time? She looked happy when I left her with Kori a couple of minutes ago. She was smiling, and she hasn't done a lot of that lately."

He wanted to be the reason she smiled every minute of the day. "We talked mostly. And touched, but nothing sexual. She needs affection. She likes to be petted. I almost wish we were having a pet night."

He would turn her into his sweet kitten, stroking her and lavishing her with affection.

"Yeah, I don't think that's up Charlotte's alley, but she and Big Tag will have a blast leading the ceremony tomorrow night. You're sure she won't see through the mask?"

It covered most of his face. He'd found without being able to see his trademark scruff a lot of people didn't recognize him. He was planning on shaving before tomorrow night. It would be fine because when he saw Sarah again his scruff would have grown back out. He did not have a problem growing facial hair. He was the guy who needed to shave twice a day. "It'll be fine. She didn't recognize my voice. She told me she's going on some kind of vacation next week."

Kai shifted, turning toward him. "Yes, it came up suddenly."

His brother was suspicious. He knew that look well. "You think she's lying?"

"I don't know. I only know that she's suddenly decided to go away to California for three weeks to see friends she's never talked about before."

"You think she's meeting someone?" The thought made him ache. Was there some man in California who had her attention now? Had she stopped talking to him so she could pursue this new man? "She told me she couldn't do a long-term relationship, but after we talked for a bit, I got her to admit she wasn't against spending time with a man. She said she needed to take things slow. She did say she wanted to travel."

"She loves to travel. She and Kori take some awesome girls' trips, and she's gone with the two of us on many occasions. It's why I'm surprised she's going by herself. Kori's tried to talk her into waiting a week or two so she could go with her, but she says she needs to go alone. Yes, I'm worried she's meeting a man. She can be reckless at times."

"I'll have a bodyguard follow her. Better yet, let's figure out exactly where she's going."

Kai's shoulders relaxed. "Thank god. I've been worried. You can do it. Kori would kill me if I did it."

"I'll talk to Big Tag tomorrow."

Kai stood and slapped him on the shoulder. "Excellent. I like having moneybags for a brother. And you're a good shield. I'll go tell Kori we're heading home. We can stop for a beer at the sports bar and try to catch the end of the Stars game."

"I thought you were going to the party." He'd been ready to spend the evening alone.

"Well, my brother's here and I should spend some time with him. Make sure he doesn't get into trouble."

He smiled, grabbed his bag, and followed his brother out.

Chapter Six

In which our hero and heroine meet in the light...and Julian Lodge is an asshole...

"You are not playing football."

Sarah glanced up from where she sat, watching as Case and Mia Taggart started walking close. Heath Taggart was held in his father's arms, a mop of blond curls around his face. He grinned and waved, utterly ignoring his parents' arguments.

Case frowned his wife's way. "It's flag football."

"And you got your ass kicked last week," Mia replied. She stopped and looked down at Sarah. "Sarah, you're a reasonable woman."

She nodded. "Which is why I stay out of Taggart family arguments. I agree with everyone and see everyone's point. Would you like a cookie?"

Mia grinned. "You are a smart woman. Okay, maybe I'm being too overly protective. Case was working at my brother's company last week. We had a corporate spy who decided to run, and Case chased him and decided to do that thing where the bad guy is running down the stairs and the good guy thinks he's a superhero and jumps over the railing."

She winced because she could see how that probably had gone. "What did he break?"

Case rolled his eyes. "I didn't break anything. I twisted my ankle a little."

"It was the size of Heath's head." Mia sent her husband the look all women sent their men when they were being dumbasses. "I get that the swelling has gone down but it's not even fully healed yet. Sarah, do you honestly believe this is a friendly game where no one gets hurt and everyone respects the physical limitations of the other players?"

Sarah felt her eyes go wide. "Oh, no. You see it starts out nice and then Big Tag and Julian start trash-talking, and it's downhill from there. I've been to most of these. I remember the year when we had it out at the Barnes-Fleetwood Ranch and someone thought it would be funny to send a bull through the field. Except it was twenty of them. There was the year Jesse joined the company and someone tackled him—accidently, of course—and we had to use a tranquilizer dart on him. We have a tranq gun. Seriously, I've been taught how to use it. I am literally here to save lives. Faith Smith makes sure she's here this weekend every year so we have a doctor on hand. Sorry, Case. That was never going to work. She's met your brother."

Case groaned. "Then she should know if I don't play he'll give me a set of pom-poms."

"And I will shove them up his ass." Mia winked Sarah's way. "I'll be back for those cookies."

She watched them walk toward the tent the Taggarts had set up. Someone—likely Ian himself—had come out early and set up a huge tent and tables and chairs. There was a barbecue thing going. There was probably some technical name for it, but all that mattered was the sweet smell coming off it. Every now and then Alex McKay would open it and flip meat over with his tongs. Then Tag would say something and Alex would obviously threaten to shove his tongs up Tag's butthole.

He got that a lot.

They were a big family and Tag was the obnoxious uncle who held everything and everyone together. She knew if she wanted to, she could walk right into that tent and be welcomed. She would be treated like family.

But she wasn't really family. Besides, it was nice to be alone for a moment. It gave her time to think.

Sarah let her head fall back, sunlight warming her face as she thought about the night before. She was sitting on a large blanket, the white color making a gorgeous contrast to the velvety green grass that made up the park. Her dress was sunny yellow, also in vibrant contrast to the white.

I'm a Dom who thinks he knows what you need.

She'd thought about Sir all night long. She'd gone to the after party, listening carefully to each voice she heard to try to identify the man she'd spent hours talking to. There had been about ten Doms she hadn't met or knew very little about. None of them had seemed like the man whose lap she'd sat on.

They'd been attractive, seemingly nice, but not a one of them had moved her, and she'd started to wonder if it had been the fact that the whole evening had been so different that made it seem like she'd been moved. Or she was overly emotional and looking for anything to cling to. That could be it.

"Is this seat taken?"

She opened her eyes and wished she'd kept them closed. Jared was standing there, looming over her like a gorgeous statue. Except no statue had his ridiculously sunny smile or those green eyes that seemed to warm the world around her. "There's a whole park. You should be able to find somewhere to sit."

His smile dimmed and he stepped back. He wore athletic pants and a T-shirt that hid what she knew was the singular most spectacular chest ever created by body building and the careful avoidance of carbs. He wore sneakers on his feet and a Seattle Seahawks cap on his head. He was scruffy and gorgeous and perfect. "Sorry. Kori said she and Kai would be with you. I'll find another place."

She was such a bitch. He was here to see his brother, who happened to be married to her best friend. She was the one who should end up alone. He was blood. She didn't have any of that in this world. "No, you should hang with Kai. It's fine. I'm sorry. I didn't think I would see you until tomorrow."

"And you didn't want to."

Oh, she wanted to see him. If he knew how many times she had watched his TV show, he would think she was a pathetic little fangirl. "I think it's safer that I don't see you, but I didn't realize you were coming today. I won't make you go and sit by yourself."

The truth was if she wanted to stay friends with Kori, it looked like she would have to deal with Jared from time to time.

It would have been so much easier if she'd never answered his call. She'd picked up because he'd stopped calling months before and she worried something had happened to Kai. He'd merely gotten lonely and tried again. She should have hung up. Instead she'd spent hours talking to him. The next time, they'd gotten on the computer and it was a little like they'd been together. She'd started to think they could work.

"I don't want to hurt you."

The man could give her the most soulful looks. It was why he'd been so successful at acting. Looking at him made her heart ache, but she simply smiled. "It's fine. Are Kai and Kori on their way?"

"Kai is talking to some guy with a ponytail very similar to his own. It's kind of like he's talking to himself," Jared said, his hands on his hips. "Kori's talking to the guy's wife, who I think might be cheating on him because she was macking down with another dude. Or they have a very open marriage."

Ah, so he'd met the other side. "That's Leo Meyer. He's The Club's version of Kai. The woman's name is Shelley and she's married to Leo and his brother, Wolf. Not legally, though. I don't think they can do that. But those Club people tend to view their world as kind of a country in and of itself. Julian Lodge is their leader and if he said kinky three-ways should be turned into a monogamous thing, then they respect it. Is it monogamy? Polygamy? I don't know. I just know Shelley Meyer probably does a shit ton of laundry."

Jared lowered himself down, keeping her fully packed picnic basket in between them. "So they're both married to her, like Jake and Adam are married to Serena?"

"Yes." She wondered how long Kori was going to take. Simply sitting with the man was making all thoughts of her lovely Sir fly straight out of her head. Jared was overpowering to her every sense. "It's a thing at The Club. Like we've got one threesome at Sanctum. They've got one couple. Big Tag says it's because they've got way smaller penises than the guys at Sanctum and it takes two to please a woman, but I happen to know that most of those threesomes are super kinky and everyone is fucking, if you know what I mean. Like Julian does both his subs. But not the brothers. I'm sure they're very respectful of each other's personal space when they have sex with their wife."

"Do Adam and Jake?" Jared's voice had gone low, conspiratorial.

She shook her head. "No. Not that I've heard. They're pretty loud when they're in a scene, and they are careful about the penises not touching."

"That's a different world," Jared said with a shake of his head as though he couldn't even fathom the thought of sharing a woman with his brother.

"You should see the guys from Bliss. Think threesomes but with aliens and sasquatches. Not that I've seen that. Just heard a rumor. And beets. What's up with the beets?"

His brows rose. "What do beets have to do with three-ways?"

God he was so gorgeous. "I have no idea. I've never been there."

A super uncomfortable silence descended. All around her the party was revving up. The men from The Club were wearing matching T-shirts in red and black. The ones who were playing, that is. They were across the soccer field that was being used for football today. Julian Lodge was as casual as he got, wearing a button-down shirt, slacks and what were probably thousand-dollar loafers that would almost certainly not see a football field today or any other day. He was wearing sunglasses and looking super-billionaire cool as he held his daughter in his arms, smiling with the glow of a proud father. He watched as his "team" began warming up.

The Sanctum crew was not as organized.

Should she say something else? She wanted to ask him how he'd been doing. The last time they'd talked he'd just gotten the word that he wasn't going to get the part he'd wanted in a major franchise. Was he struggling? Did he have another show? He should be in every movie, but she'd heard Kai talk about the fact that there were still rumors he was a killer.

Stupid assholes. He was as far from a killer as possible. The only thing that man could slay was hearts.

"I heard you were going on a vacation."

She plastered a sunny smile on her face. "Next week. I'll be gone for three whole weeks."

Three weeks alone, but that was how it had to be. She didn't have anyone, and she wasn't about to make Kori worry.

"Are you seeing friends?"

"I'm taking a sabbatical. I'll make friends." She didn't want to think about this now. She got to her knees and opened the picnic basket. It was a universal truth that if a woman wanted a man to stop talking, she should put something in his mouth. "Do you want a sandwich? I have ham and swiss, turkey and American, and pimento cheese." She hadn't planned on him being here. "Sorry. I could get rid of the bread. I have some napkins."

He shook his head. "Oh, I'm good with carbs. I'm not training for anything right now so I'm happily eating like a real human. I had a donut this morning. It was chocolate. I'd love the ham and swiss."

She reached in and grabbed one of the ham and swiss sandwiches she'd made. The basket was full of treats, including her famous snickerdoodles. She'd spent the morning putting it together, wondering if the mysterious Sir would show up and need some food.

She couldn't quite remember what his voice sounded like now.

"Thanks. Getting to eat is a definite plus of being unemployed." He ate half the sandwich in a single bite.

She sat back and hoped she had enough food. "I'm sure you'll get another show soon."

He shrugged. "I'm okay, Sarah. I'm enjoying the time off. It's given me space to think about a lot of things."

"I thought you were working on the documentary." It was supposed to be the whole reason he was here.

"I am, but that doesn't feel like work. It's more than that. Are you still okay with talking about it?"

"Yes." She'd thought about it a lot. "I think you might be able to do something good. None of us saw anything wrong with Squirrel. I know I didn't spend much time with him, but I wouldn't have thought anything was wrong. He seemed normal, with the exception of his name."

"I spent most of my life with him. I knew he could be an asshole about women. I always thought he would chill when the right one came along."

"You know he was a sociopath, right?" The idea that he'd been blaming himself made her ache. She'd known he did in the beginning, but shouldn't time and distance have shown him he was innocent? "He would have been excellent at hiding his true nature."

"He wasn't that smart," Jared insisted.

"Or he was and he was excellent at hiding it," she pointed out.

"The funny thing was one of the reasons I stayed around him was I got to be the smart one." Jared put down the sandwich. "Kai was always so much smarter than I was. I didn't hate him for it. I loved my brother, but I will admit that hanging out with Squirrel made me feel like I got to be in charge. I got to be the one someone looked up to."

She didn't want him to devolve. "I think this isn't the time or place to talk about this. If you keep going, I'll cry and then my mascara will go everywhere. Do you want to be responsible for that? I'll frighten the children with my raccoon eyes."

"No," he said quietly. "I wouldn't want to do that. I've missed you."

Of course she also didn't want to talk about this, either. "I've been gone a long time. Or I guess you've been gone. I didn't actually go anywhere."

"I shouldn't have left."

"I think it was for the best." At the time she'd been devastated. It felt like the end of the world. Now she knew better. Now she knew what it felt like when the world ended.

"It wasn't best for me." He looked out over the field. "They look happy. Everyone here looks happy."

The longing in his voice pulled at her heart. She knew that same longing. "I'm sure you know lots of happy people."

"Fewer than you would think. I know the image is of glitz and glamour and everyone thinks if they just had money and fame everything else would fall in line. It doesn't work that way. Money isn't love. Money isn't family. Fame isn't happiness. You go into the whole fame thing thinking this is the way I get love. When all these people love me, then I'll be worthy."

"Jared," she began.

He shook his head. "It's okay. I know what I was doing back then. I was looking for acceptance. I was looking for affection. The trouble was not a one of those people knew me. They loved an actor who smiled and showed off his abs. They didn't know I missed my brother. They didn't know what haunts me at night or what I want for the future. I was a pretty face, a nice body, an aspirational ideal. I was a fantasy, and I'm no fantasy man, as you found out."

She sighed and wished she could reach out to him, but that was a bad idea. "You were always a real man to me, Jared."

He chuckled, but it wasn't a humorous sound. "I doubt that."

"What is that supposed to mean?"

He stared at her for a moment as though trying to decide if he wanted to reply. "Sarah, you watched me work out like it was meant to entertain you. All we talked about when we met was Hollywood crap and who I knew and what kind of parties I went to. It was a fantasy I wanted to take further because you blew me away the moment I laid eyes on you. One of the reasons I walked away was because I knew how hard it would be on you if I let the fantasy become real."

Had she made him feel like he was a piece of really gorgeous meat? In the beginning she'd seen him as something of a conquest. She couldn't help it. He was one of those men who wasn't quite real. He was far too perfect. "At first I thought I could steal a couple of days with you and then I would be able to tell my friends, yep, I bagged him."

"You wouldn't be the only one," he pointed out.

"I'm sorry if I made you feel that way. I wouldn't want to feel like no one knew the real me." She hadn't even thought of it. She'd seen him as a gorgeous piece of man meat, a prize to be won. Something that had slipped from her fingers. "If it helps, I don't think of you that way now."

"I don't think you think of me at all." He stared out over the field. "Could you tell me what I said? What I did to make you stop talking to me? I thought we were becoming friends."

The whole world seemed to fade away, leaving only the two of them. "Is that what you wanted? To be my friend?"

"No. That's never what I've wanted from you. I wanted more. I want more."

"I can't give it to you." It was the "more" part that she couldn't do. The forever, happily ever after part.

"Is it because I'm not working much anymore?"

The words were a kick to her gut. "No. Not at all. I think we were getting to be friends."

"Don't you want to know?" He didn't make a single move to close in on her, but those eyes of his pinned her. "I've spent every day since I met you wanting to know."

He didn't have to say the words. She knew exactly what he meant. Didn't she want to know what it would feel like to have his arms around her? To lie beneath him while he thrust inside her? Didn't she want to know what it felt like to make love to Jared Johns? The trouble was she didn't care what it felt like to make love to the movie star anymore. She could have handled that. It was the man who moved her, the man who made her want things she couldn't have.

She should tell him she wasn't curious, that she had no interest in him sexually. "Of course I do."

"Then why did you stop talking to me?"

She was so tired.

He got to his knees in front of her. "I'm sorry I asked. You don't owe me a reason."

But they'd been getting so close. If he'd been the one to stop taking her calls, she would want a reason, too.

She hadn't said good-bye to him. She hadn't given him a moment's closure. Why? Why hadn't she simply gotten him on the phone and lied to him? She could have told him any story, but she hadn't. "I think I was punishing you. It wasn't fair of me."

Untrue. She hadn't been punishing him. She was saving them both pain. Or putting off the inevitable because telling him the truth might sway her choice. Being with him might make her think she could put it off, wait a few years. What could it hurt?

He was staring at her with those gorgeous eyes. "I don't want to hurt you. Do you want me to leave? I can send someone to tape your interview. It doesn't have to be me."

Was she willing to never see him again? He was her best friend's brother-in-law. Kori and Kai had become her family in the last few years. Jared needed his family, too. "Don't leave. You belong here as much as I do. I think that might be another reason I pulled away from you. If we did get together and it went wrong somewhere down the line, what would happen then?"

"What do you mean?"

"I mean you're Kai's brother. If we break up, I'm on the outside," she explained.

"I would never leave you on the outside."

"What about holidays? I spend them with Kori and Kai. How would you feel about spending Thanksgiving with your ex-girlfriend? If we break up, one of us loses our family, and it seems like it's too much to risk. Neither one of us has another family."

"I hadn't thought about it that way. But I'm not a vindictive person, Sarah. If for some reason we broke up, I would never push you out. I wouldn't. I would try very hard to find a way to be friends with you." He relaxed back, closer to her now than he'd been before. "I care about you. That won't stop because you pull away from me. Until you tell me to leave you alone, I'm probably going to keep trying to get you to talk to me. I want you badly. I might play dirty."

There was nothing she wanted more from this man than to see how dirty he could play. "But you would leave me alone if I told you to."

His eyes became grave. "I would."

She couldn't do it. It wasn't fair. She was planning on seeing another man later tonight. She was interested in Sir. Sir might be someone she could have an actual relationship with, even if it was merely a D/s relationship. It would be something, some connection she could rely on.

"I don't want you to go, but I can't promise you anything." The right words simply wouldn't come out of her mouth. "And you should know I'm seeing someone at Sanctum. It's only for the weekend, for Charlotte's party. Did Kai tell you about that?"

"He mentioned there was a big celebration going on at the club." He downed the rest of the sandwich.

"Sanctum." She had to be precise.

He nodded. "Yeah, the club. Wait. Is this about the other club? It's very confusing."

She couldn't help but grin. "I think Master Julian likes it that way."

He smiled back. God, when that boy smiled he was brighter than the sun. "I'll have to go see it sometime. The Club, that is. My friend has a membership there. He couldn't get into Sanctum. I guess he didn't know the right people."

Oh, he could flirt. He could flirt for hours, and every word out of his mouth made her heart pound. "I don't know. Some people think Julian Lodge is pretty powerful."

"I'm too used to the way Big Tag does things," he admitted. "I'm going to have to be Team Sanctum all the way. Maybe someday I'll even be a regular."

What if they could have a D/s relationship? What if they sat down and went over a very explicit contract that described their roles and what they could expect from the other? They could go over protocols of what had to happen if they chose to break up. If they went into it being honest and forthright, maybe she wouldn't get hurt. Maybe. She needed time to think about it. She couldn't make a decision here and now. "So do you want to try for the friends thing? For now?"

In a few weeks she would have a better handle on what her life would look like. She would have had time to examine how she felt. She would know what to tell him.

The most delicious expression crept across his face. It was a mischievous expression, the kind that said *I'm going to tell you what you want and still try to have you.* He held his hand out. "Friends it is."

The minute she touched him her whole body seemed to spark. She knew it wasn't real. It was nothing but her own reaction to his insane charm, but when she touched him it felt like the world lit up.

"Are you the guy from TV?"

She looked to her left and there was a full gang of kiddos standing in front of them. The Taggart twins were front and center, but they were joined by Olivia and Josh Barnes-Fleetwood, Carys Taggart and Chloe

Lodge. A massive mutt of a dog sat beside them. Kenzie held his leash, but Bud was a well-trained pup. He simply followed the Taggart twins around, happily wagging his tail at everyone he greeted.

Unlike a lot of single guys she knew, Jared didn't seem uncomfortable around a bunch of kids. He gave them a steady smile. "I was on TV for a while. I played a guy named Dart."

"My dad says darts can't kill people," one of the Tag twins said. "But I think anything can kill if you hit something hard enough with it."

She was pretty sure that was Kala. Kala scared her. One time she'd been at a Christmas party and someone had given the twins a matching set of bouncing giraffes to ride on. Kenzie had squealed with delight and promptly started bouncing around the party. Kala had taken the toy by the neck and disappeared like a lion dragging prey. She still wasn't sure what had happened to that giraffe.

"What about marshmallows?" Olivia asked, looking at the younger girl, her arms crossed over her chest. Olivia looked an awful lot like her momma, Abby Barnes-Fleetwood. "I don't think a marshmallow could kill anything."

Jared shrugged. "It could if you were allergic to marshmallows. Or if you got a hundred thousand of them and drowned a person in them."

Kala nodded as though the image was going through her young brain and she found it pleasing. "Yes, I can see that."

"Do you know Spongebob?" Kenzie asked with a bright smile.

"I haven't had the pleasure, but I do know a couple of Pokémon," Jared replied.

"No way," Carys said, obviously impressed.

"Yes, way." Jared turned to Sarah, giving her a wink. "I know some of the actors who do the voices."

Josh Barnes-Fleetwood had a cowboy hat on his head and a cynical look on his young face. She'd been told he was six, but he always seemed older to her. "Well, I don't see what the fuss is about. He doesn't look like a bull to me."

Carys nodded. "He doesn't. Momma said he was probably a bull in bed, but I don't know what that means."

Bud's tail thumped against the ground as if he didn't understand either.

Jared was overtaken by a sudden coughing fit.

"I think she means he's probably really strong." Sarah fought back a laugh. "He works out a lot."

Josh stared at Jared like he might or might not be a threat. "My dads work out in the gym. Not the bedroom."

"Oh, I bet your dads..." She was going to say that she was pretty sure there was some serious working out going down at the ranch, but a big hand covered her mouth and Jared was laughing as he held her close.

"She was going to say that all dads work out in their gyms," Jared managed over his laughter. He had one arm wrapped around her waist and the other over her mouth. "That's all, and I am pretty strong. From working out. In a gym."

"Nicely done, Johns." Big Tag strode up, a football in his hand. "Kids, leave the civvies alone. They have no idea how to handle you. Go on. I think you'll find the hot dogs are ready and there's brownies for you afterward. Let me take Bud or he'll end up eating a bunch of the hot dogs and barfing everywhere."

Kenzie handed over the leash and the kids raced off, with the exception of Kala who stood in front of her dad. He knelt down and gave her a smile. "You okay, kid?"

Her lips turned up and she leaned over and whispered something in her dad's ear.

Big Tag nodded. "I'll think about it. It's an interesting idea. Go on, kiddo."

She ran off to join her sister.

Big Tag stood up, looming over them. "Why does my daughter now want to find a way to weaponize marshmallows?"

Jared, eased back, his arms loosening. "I think that's my fault. She was trying to convince the other kids that anything could be a weapon if placed in the right hands. I was kind of backing her up."

Tag nodded. "That's a good move on your part. I'm pretty sure she's keeping a list. It wasn't such a big deal when I thought she would forget, but now that she can write, it's getting real, if you know what I mean. Let's go, Johns. We're going to get this game going. You're my secret weapon."

Jared scrambled to get up. "You know I haven't played in a long time."

"Yeah, that's okay. You're the new guy and our wives watch your work-out porn. While the other team chases you around trying to rough you up, we're going to score. This is going to be the best year ever."

Jared stared at the big guy. "Maybe we should talk about this."

"I think you'll be great," Sarah said. If he was going to play, the game had just gotten way more interesting.

He glanced down and she watched as his face became resolute. "I'll see you after?"

What was she going to do about him? "I'll save some cookies."

"I would love that."

He looked like he might have stayed, but Big Tag started to drag him along with the dog. "Cookies are for after. I need you hungry on the field. Let's go kick some ass. Well, I'll kick ass. You'll probably get your ass kicked."

Jared looked back at her, his eyes almost pleading.

He was even sexy when he was desperate.

"Where's Jared going?" Kori walked up, three dogs on her heels. They were on leashes and kind of running every which way they wanted. "I thought he was planning on trying to talk to you. He told me he would ask your permission to sit with us. I texted you a heads-up. Are you mad at me?"

How could she be mad when there were French bulldogs? She pulled Gideon onto her lap. "Hello, sweetheart. How are you? And no, I'm not mad at your mom." She held the dog close to her heart as she looked up at her bestie. "It's fine. We've decided to be friends."

Kori sighed and dropped down to the blanket. "I'm so glad. He's lonely. I don't want to have to ask him to stay away."

It wasn't fair to make him keep his distance. It was his family. Was she doing the right thing keeping her secret from them all? Was she doing it for the reason she told herself she was—to spare them the worry? Or was she doing it because she was worried they wouldn't worry much at all?

"You think I won't wear this, Lodge?" Big Tag's voice boomed across the field. "Because this is a damn badge of honor, asshole!"

"Ian, children!" Charlotte yelled, just as loud.

He turned and grinned. "Yeah, baby, this is where they come from."

He pointed to his shirt.

Kori squinted. "Does that say what I think it says?"

Sarah nodded. "Yep. Yep, it does. Someone doesn't know how to spell."

Or they knew how to prank. It was exactly the type of thing she expected out of one of these events. She watched as Jared pulled his shirt over his head and for a moment his chest came into view. His stunningly sculpted chest with its ridiculous eight pack and notched hips that led to what she suspected was an amazingly beautiful penis. She couldn't help but sigh.

"Let the games begin."

* * * *

"You think about telling her the truth?" Big Tag asked as they walked toward the tent where it appeared the "team" had gathered.

Bud lumbered beside them and Jared was reminded again of how much he missed having a dog.

"About what I'm doing at night while I'm here? I've thought about it. I don't know if it will make her think I'm honest or if she'll kick my ass to the curb. I think I need more time. I still don't know exactly what's going on with her. She says she's worried about what happens if we become a couple and then we break up. Kori and Kai are her only family."

"That's not true. She's got a large family if she wants it. Sanctum is her family. She simply hasn't figured that out yet and until she does, telling her won't mean a thing." Big Tag strode past the tent where a bunch of kids were now eating hot dogs and joined the big group of Sanctum guys who were tossing a football around or helping each other stretch. "Bud, stay."

He put the leash down and Bud simply yawned and laid himself out on the grass. There was absolutely no thought in that dog's head to running away. He was right where he wanted to be.

It must be nice.

"Have you tried telling her she has a family?" There was a large box sitting on one of the picnic tables that dotted the park.

"Do you think we don't invite her to family functions? She's always welcome," Tag explained. "The problem is sometimes when you lose your family like Sarah did, it can be hard to get used to depending on people again. The sad truth of the human state is loneliness is easier for some of us. It feels right to be alone even when we hate it. When those people who cared about us most in the world are gone, it doesn't matter how many people say they love us until we believe it for ourselves. You know she lost her mom at a pretty young age, right?"

Big Tag picked up a box cutter that had been left on the table and cut through the tape holding the box closed.

"I know she's alone. Both of her parents died. Her mom before her dad."

"Her mom died when Sarah was in her teens. Ovarian cancer," Big Tag said. "Her father died a few years ago. He had a heart attack. She didn't have any siblings and her blood family was spread out across the country. So she found her club family. That works most of the time, but I suspect holidays are rough on her. We can invite her, but she needs a place of her own. I think we'll always be extended family to her and that's great. But she needs a family of her own however she can get it."

He wanted to be her family, but it made sense that she would be afraid she could lose the only one she had. Was that why she was going on this trip? Was she trying to figure out how to be alone? "I would never keep her from Kori and Kai."

"No, but you're blood and she's not, and blood is a tricky thing." Tag opened the box and pulled out a bunch of black T-shirts with purple lettering. "Personally, I think we put too much emphasis on it. Alex is as much my brother as Sean, Case, and Theo. I would do anything for him, and these kids we're all raising, well, they're my family, too. Sarah needs to understand she's a part of this. She has been for years. She hides behind that Disney princess thing she's got going. She's afraid if she decides on what she wants, the evil queen will show up and take it away from her. After all, it's already happened once."

"There was an evil queen? Who? She never mentioned a woman trying to hurt her."

Tag shook his head. "We're lucky you're so pretty, man. It's a metaphor. Cancer is the evil queen, and she rears her head at the worst of times. Sarah was a perfectly happy teenager, from what I can tell, and then she was a daughter mourning her mom. Men don't deal with things the way women do. I would bet her father distanced after her mother died and she felt like she was alone in the world. Not that I think about it a lot. Those are just surface opinions."

Yeah, he wasn't that dumb. Big Tag thought about his people all the time. He treated the members of his club like family, and the fact that Sarah didn't have any blood relations would make him more protective of her. She'd been a sub at Sanctum for a very long time, had been one of the first to join who wasn't a McKay-Taggart employee. Big Tag cared about her and that meant Jared should listen. "You think I should tell her I'm the man she spent last night with?"

"I think you should tread carefully because something's going on with her, something serious. If you care about her, you'll be careful with her."

"I love her." He'd known for a long time, but it felt good to say it out loud.

"I did not need to know that, man." Big Tag swallowed like he was containing his vomit. "Just think about it."

"I can't not think about it. I wonder if I'm being selfish. I didn't take her with me when things were good. Now that they're shitty, here I am trying to coax her to my side."

"Or you could view it as you went out, got your money, and now you're going to ditch the crappy stuff and have an awesome life with your lady. Do you worry about paparazzi anymore? Does it bother you that photographers don't chase after you constantly?"

He shuddered. "That was cool for five minutes. I feel for my friend Josh. They're all over him and Kay constantly. I didn't want that for Sarah. She's gorgeous, but I've seen those tabloids take down even the most confident of women."

"Now you don't have to worry about it."

"But I do have to worry about other things. I've traded the paparazzi for trolls."

One big shoulder shrugged. "She can handle it if she wants you. If she doesn't, it's a great excuse. What the fuck?"

He held up the T-shirt and frowned.

SANTCUM

Yeah, even he knew that wasn't spelled right.

Big Tag pulled his shirt off and tugged the new one on before turning to where Julian Lodge stood. "You think I won't wear this, Lodge? Because this is a damn badge of honor, asshole!"

Everyone stopped, looking their way.

"Ian, children!" Charlotte jogged up to them.

Big Tag turned to his wife. "Yeah, baby, this is where they come from."

He pointed to his shirt and Charlotte slapped a hand over her mouth.

Julian Lodge strode up, two big men on either side of him. Twins. "Something is wrong with your shirts, Taggart. Did you have trouble spelling the name of your club correctly?"

Jared looked back and sure enough, Sarah had her eyes on him.

"I think Chase there hacked into the T-shirt place and replaced my perfectly spelled design with this one," Tag shot back. "Bud, kill."

Bud's head came up but he merely started wagging his tail as the man named Chase knelt down in front of him. Bud popped up and started enthusiastically licking the man.

"Yep, you got a killer here, Tag," he said, petting the massive mutt.

"I know where his tongue has been. Don't think death is off the table yet," Tag replied. "And I like the shirt. It's awesome."

Sarah was still watching. Him. Maybe it was time to give her a little of what he knew she liked. He might have been eating a few more carbs, but he still looked good. He tugged at the back of his shirt and eased it over his head. The athletic pants he wore rode low on his hips, showing off the notches he'd worked so hard for. He stretched—after all he was about to perform athletic feats of getting his ass kicked, so he should stretch.

Sarah's eyes had gone wide, and even from where he was standing he could see the way she bit her bottom lip.

He still had it.

"Ian, I didn't have Chase screw up your shirts," Julian said with a chuckle. "I have my own secret weapon. I certainly don't need to misspell the name of your club."

"Chase did it all on his own," Ian accused.

"I did it." Adam Miles stepped up, his hands on his hips. "And the rest of them are spelled correctly. Just yours is fucked up."

The world seemed to still as though two long-term adversaries had finally met on the field of battle and war was about to rage.

Then Ian threw his head back and his laugh boomed across the field. "Oh, that's awesome, man. Adam, this is a classic prank. Seriously, somebody get me a sharpie. I love this so much fucking much."

Someone handed Big Tag a black pen and he quickly added and "i" so the shirt read—*SAiNTCUM*.

"Now I'm Saint Cum, and we know it's true because Charlie's knocked up again," Ian said with a big grin.

Adam simply shook his head, his shoulders slumping. "Last week I sent him a giant chocolate dick with a card that said 'eat a dick.' Do you know what he did?"

"It was chocolate," Ian replied. "It was delicious. Next time, make sure to fill it with cream so it kind of shoots out the head. It's okay. You'll get there, buddy."

Charlotte slapped her husband's arm. "You have to give him

something, Ian."

Big Tag shrugged. "I told him it was an awesome prank. Baby, it's not my fault I genuinely love pranks and they're cool. He's the one who leaves his goat right in the middle of the lawn with a big old sign that says 'please get me.'"

Julian Lodge simply chuckled. "He should know you aren't one to be embarrassed. Chase, that dog likely licks his own ass. Aren't you supposed to be a germaphobe? Let's go and get this started. I want to get to the fun part of the day. Ah, my surprise is here. This, Mr. Miles, is how you get Taggart's goat to come out and play."

A thudding sound came from above and then all eyes were on the helicopter descending in the middle of the park.

He looked at Tag and sure enough, his face was turning a nice shade of red. "I thought there was a storm in Colorado."

Julian shrugged, an elegant motion. "Where there's a will, there's always a way. Gentlemen, meet our quarterback for this game. Hello, Trevor!"

A man hopped out of the chopper, slinging his bag over one broad shoulder.

"Is that who I think it is?" Jared couldn't stop staring.

Big Tag practically seethed. "Trevor McNamara. He used to play in the pros and now he gets his balls kicked by cattle and he's supposed to be in Colorado."

The chopper took off again, having deposited its cargo. The former pro was dressed to play in sweats and a T-shirt. "Sorry I'm late."

"I'm sorry you're here," Tag shot back.

"He's sorry that his secret weapon isn't as good as my secret weapon," Julian said with a smooth smile. "Mr. Johns, it's lovely to meet you. Please know you're welcome at The Club anytime. Ian, see you on the field. Well, my men will. And Mistress Katherine. I would be careful of her if I was you."

"Yeah, well Erin will take her out," Tag promised.

"No, she won't," Theo yelled back. "Erin's pregnant, too."

"Damn it. Our sperm curses us every time." Tag shook his head. "I still stand behind this shirt!"

McNamara strode up and held out a hand. "Hello. Julian told me you would be here. You're the actor, right?"

How did he answer that question now? He was and he wasn't. He was now, probably wasn't in the future. "I'm Jared."

"Trev," he said, shaking his hand. "Good to meet you." His eyes narrowed. "You should put on a shirt. You always find a way to take your shirt off. You need a shirt here. And keep those pants on, too. My wife's a big fan. Not that she likes any other TV shows."

He strode off.

Big Tag put a hand on his shoulder as the other guys started putting on their properly spelled shirts. "Excellent. His wife thinks you're hot. He probably wants to kill you. That should throw off his accuracy. This can still work. You don't have any darts on you, do you? Because if you wanted to throw a few Julian's way, go for it."

He strode off to get his team ready.

Jared was left with Bud and a shirt that didn't quite fit.

The day was not looking up.

Thirty minutes later, Jared grinned as he neatly evaded one of the Dawson twins and landed firmly in the end zone.

The crowd around him cheered and he glanced over to see Sarah on her feet. She was the only woman in the crowd wearing heels and she somehow managed to walk across the thick grass without sinking into it. She stood out to him, so much more beautiful than the rest.

He was more certain than ever that she was the woman for him. He winked her way and was more than satisfied with the blush that came across her cheeks.

They'd gathered a crowd that went far beyond the members of each club. Apparently word had gotten out that former pro quarterback Trev McNamara was playing football in the park and the crowd had doubled.

"Doing good, Johns," Alex McKay said, taking the football from him and passing it over to the other side. "We only need to score three more times and we might be able to claim moral victory. I told Ian we needed to appeal to more kinky pro athletes. Damn McNamara hasn't lost a step."

He hadn't. Jared had found himself staring at how the man dropped out of the pocket, his arm moving back as though the football was a mere reflection of his will. That football went where McNamara wanted it to go.

"I think we'll have to be happy just to have played today, man," he admitted. But it was a beautiful day. The sky above him was a stunning blue and the weather was warm with a hint of crisp wind to cool things off.

This could be his life. His life with Sarah. Their kids could be the ones running around with a big dog at their sides, playing like they didn't have a care in the world. It would be safe to have a family here because his children would never be alone. Even if something happened to him and Sarah, his brother and Kori would make sure they had good lives, people who loved and supported them.

He could have this.

"You kill any women lately, Johns?"

He stopped at the shouted question. The words were ugly, insidious, and they stripped away the brilliant light of the day and sent him looking for the shadows.

Big Tag was yelling something, but he couldn't make the words out.

"You're the one who should be in jail!"

He turned and caught sight of a man. He barely registered what the man looked like. It didn't matter. He was one of the people who seemed to follow him around. He wasn't sure how he'd found him here. Probably someone had recognized him and posted his location online. It had been months since one of them challenged him in person. They usually preferred to make their accusations online, but every now and then one would come out of the shadows and confront him, and it got nasty.

His first instinct was to get in the man's face. He didn't have the right to come here. This was his private life. The need to show the fucker just how he killed a person was right there bubbling under the surface. It was different when he was confronted by someone who'd known one of the women who died. He would take that. He would try to talk to those people, to let them know he heard their pain.

This was a troll, someone who'd decided he was the enemy, and trolls needed enemies. Trolls needed something to torment, to punch and kick and take out their anger on.

"Hey, you okay?" Alex asked.

"Do you know you're playing with a killer? He raped and tortured women," the man yelled.

He looked around and his friends were starting to realize something was wrong. Sarah had her hands over her eyes, trying to get a look at what was going on. The kids. God, the kids would hear this crap and be afraid. Afraid of him. Afraid of words they shouldn't have to know yet.

He'd brought this here.

"You got something to say?" Alex stepped up.

If he let this continue, it would end in a fight he couldn't win. It would ruin the whole day.

"I'm going to go. It'll solve the problem," he said, stepping away.

"Or we can escort that fucker out of here," Alex promised.

And then the cops would come out. There would be explanations and reporters. They would want to talk to these very private people. "Please don't make this worse than it has to be."

"Jared, no one wants you to leave," Alex said.

The others were coming up behind him. He had very few moments to save any of the afternoon. "I got this. I don't want the cops and the press out here."

"I assure you the cops won't be here for you," Alex replied.

He shook his head. "I want to go."

He strode right past the asshole, knowing he would follow. He could lead the guy away from the happy family function.

"Where you going, Johns? You got another girl to kill?" The man did exactly what he thought he would. He followed Jared out to the parking lot and to the place where Kai had parked his Jeep.

He wasn't even sure where he would go. He'd come with Kai. His brother had the keys to the car. He could probably outrun the fucker, but where would he go?

"Back the fuck off my brother or I swear I won't care who the hell you are, I'll bury you," a deep voice said.

He turned and his brother was there.

The troll stopped, sneering Kai's way. "Hell of a family you have."

Kai's face had gone cold. "You better believe it, and some of them are figuring out exactly who you are. You might expect a visit and very soon."

"That sounds like a threat," the troll replied.

"It's a promise. I'll know your name and where you live by the end of the day. Expect a restraining order and a visit from the police," Kai said. "If you don't leave my brother alone after that, you can expect a visit from me. Do I make myself clear?"

The man backed away. "Man's got a right to his opinion."

"And I've got a right to shove your opinion up your ass." Kai unlocked the Jeep. "Get in the car, Jared. I need a beer."

His brother. In that moment he was ten again and standing behind his big brother, thinking Kai was the whole world and as long as he had

Kai, he would be okay. He was older now, knew that Kai couldn't fix everything, but god, it felt good to not be alone.

Jared got in the car.

And wondered if he had any right to drag Sarah into his life.

Chapter Seven

In which masks are put on...

Hours later Jared wasn't sure he should even be in the club.

"I heard Big Tag has to clean the restrooms at The Club for a week," JT was saying. "I don't know that I would trust him to do that. Have they seen some of the pranks he pulls?"

Sanctum had lost the game. It wasn't such a surprise since The Club had a former pro leading its team. And Sanctum had...well, if there was a dart throwing contest it would have been Lodge cleaning up. Big Tag should think about that next time.

Or a contest for who could attract the most trolls. He would win that one, too.

"Hey, you okay? I heard you had some asshole bugging you at the game. I was working, but my assistant got gooey about some pictures on the Internet. I saw one of them and it was you. I didn't realize you were some big star. I'll admit, I don't watch a bunch of TV."

He'd seen the pictures. Someone had taken cell phone pics of him and uploaded them to the Internet. The tabloids, always looking for new content, had run the photos and given away his location.

"I'm not a big star." He was well aware that his relevancy now had to do with scandal and crime, not his acting. "I used to be on a TV show and then a friend of mine turned out to be a psycho. The media loved the story. 'Hollywood star involved in killing spree' was a great headline."

"I thought we talked about this." Kai sat down on the bench beside him. His brother had basically made the afternoon one long therapy session. "You are not at fault. That man had no right to hurl those accusations your way."

"I still have to deal with the fact that a lot of people are going to and I'm dragging you into it." It was the argument he'd made all day. He looked at JT. "I should have explained my past to you. I shouldn't have offered you friendship without letting you know what it would cost. There are people out there who think I'm a killer."

JT frowned. "I run an oil company. You think I don't get my share of trolls? Hell, I've had feds up my ass making sure I dot every *I*, cross every *T* and save every turtle in the ocean since I was a kid. Living a blameless life in the age of social media doesn't exist. Every single one of us is guilty in someone's head."

Put like that, it made sense. Kai had talked around and around about how people didn't connect anymore and the anonymity of the Internet. He'd gone on about societal dysfunction. "Huh, I guess that sucks for you."

JT nodded. "Sucks for you, too. Ain't gonna stop living because of it."

Jared felt his spirits lift. "No. That would be giving in."

Kai stared at him for a moment. "Are you fucking kidding me? I just said that to you not an hour ago and you had no response."

That wasn't the way he remembered the conversation. "No, you said something about disaffected loners and the isolating cost of something. JT said it sucks and I shouldn't give in. He's right."

Kai's jaw tensed and he shook his head. "I'm so glad you're pretty."

Jared grinned. "See, I know you all think that's an insult, but I'm okay with it. I'm very comfortable being attractive. You can be the smart one." He felt better because it was good to remember that everyone had these problems and they somehow got through it, but he wasn't sure he had the right to drag Sarah into them. "I still don't know what to do about Sarah."

"Sarah?" JT asked. "The pretty lady who wears the pinup dresses and runs around with Kori? I'm going to be honest. I wouldn't hate for her to turn out to be Sweetie."

Oh, hell no. "She's not your sub. She's mine."

JT put his hands up, taking a short step back that made Jared wonder how aggressive he was being. "Hey, no problem. But I thought we didn't know who our subs are. Isn't that the whole point of this thing? We get matched up and see if it works after we go into it with no set expectations. You sound like you have a lot of expectations."

He'd had a ton of them. "I expected to walk away with Sarah. Now I think I should tell her good-bye. She doesn't need this shit in her life."

"She's stronger than you're giving her credit for," Kai argued. "Let her make the choice."

"How did you know you would get Sarah?" JT asked.

That was the simplest question of all. He'd cheated. "Because Kai does the matching and he knows I love her. I've loved her for a long time and this is probably our last shot. Now that I'm about to go out there and see if she chooses me, I realize I'm not letting her choose me. I'm lying to her. I'm manipulating things and sneaking around to get her. I'm playing dirty."

"Sometimes you have to," JT said. "Look, man, if you love her, do what you have to do, but you started this for a reason. Why did you decide to go this route?"

"Because she wouldn't talk to me."

JT frowned. "So you decided to be a stalker. That's generally frowned upon in this day and age."

"He's not a stalker." Kai defended him for the second time that day. "Sarah agreed to be paired with a compatible Dom. Jared is absolutely who I would put her with. She's a difficult placement. She needs a very indulgent Dom, one who takes the lifestyle seriously when they're playing and not at all when they're not. Jared is more than willing to let her take the lead in certain aspects of their lives. He also is capable of putting his foot down when she needs him to, and she is capable of doing the same for him. They would make an excellent married couple. I have no hesitations putting them together. That is exactly what Sarah signed up for. The only shady shit I've pulled is to let Jared know it's her. I had to do that or he wouldn't have participated."

"I wouldn't have." There was no other woman he wanted to see, no relationship he wished to get a feel for. There was only her, and it had been that way for a long time. "She's the only reason I'm in this club. I won't say I haven't played. I belong to a club in Malibu and I've done my duty. But there's been nothing sexual. I haven't so much as kissed a woman since I met Sarah."

"Okay, I can understand that." JT turned to face Kai. "What about me and Sweetie? Why did you pair us up? Because you think we're a perfect couple?"

Kai went tense again. "I think you are very compatible right now."

JT's eyes narrowed. "Why?"

"Do you honestly want to know?" Kai asked the question like he knew what the answer should be.

JT gave it a moment's thought. "Probably not, but I'm curious. Having heard you say that, my head will go a hundred different ways unless I know the truth, and a whole bunch of them will be bad."

Kai nodded, obviously accepting the answer as a valid one. "She's perfect because neither one of you is ready for a real relationship. She's younger than you, new to the lifestyle. She needs some freedom to explore and you'll give her that because you won't get serious about her."

JT stared at him. "How do you know that?"

"Because you're not ready," Kai replied. "There are things that have happened in your past that you haven't let go of and until you do, you won't be ready for anything real. You'll try with this woman, but in a few days, you'll realize it's nothing but fun and games and when she wants to date around, you'll be okay with it. That's why I put you together."

"Yeah, that's fair." JT was quiet for a moment. "You think Sweetie really won't fall for me?"

"I could be wrong, but I don't think she's ready to fall for anyone. I think she wants to have fun. I think she wants to have sex and find some friends and get her life started. You're a good bet because you won't get possessive with her," Kai pointed out. "If I put Sarah with anyone else, my caveman brother would lose his shit. But this is it. If she won't come around, he's going to let her go."

The thought made him sick inside. "I have to give her the choice. I can't let her pick me tonight if she doesn't know what or who she's picking."

"Or you can put on your mask and allow this process to work the way it's supposed to. Take a couple of days without the baggage between you. Let her find her way back to you," Kai urged.

He glanced down at the mask he'd been given at the start of this journey. It was a deep purple, and she would only be able to see his eyes and his lips. She would wear a veil this evening, something light and frothy to cover her face while she danced for the "sultan" of her choice. According to the rules of the game, she would know what color the Dom she'd been paired with would be wearing. She would make her decision and they would spend the rest of the evening playing to their hearts' content if she chose to move forward.

How could he pull her into his arms and play with her when she didn't know who he was? She thought he was some guy without his baggage, some guy who wouldn't drag her down into the mud with him.

He'd promised he would join her after the game and he'd walked out. Again. He'd texted her and said something had come up and he would see her tomorrow. She hadn't replied.

"What are you going to do?" JT asked. "I think I'm going to do what the doc here says and have fun. Maybe he's right. I think I'm ready for something I'm not, and I need to go with the flow for a while."

"You think I should go out there and not tell her the truth?"

"I think your brother knows what he's doing, but the decision has to be yours," JT replied.

"It does, Jared. You have to live with it and anything that might come from it." Kai stood up and opened his locker. "But know that no matter what you do or what happens between the two of you, I'm always your brother."

"If Sarah doesn't choose me, I need you to know that I'll stay away for a while. She needs you and Kori. It's more important for her to be comfortable." He couldn't stand the thought of her being alone.

"You need us, too," Kai said quietly.

He'd been thinking about this all day. "I think I need to know she's okay more than I need to be okay. Does that make sense?"

Kai turned to him, putting a brotherly hand on his shoulder. "It makes perfect sense and I'll always take care of her. I would do it because she's my wife's best friend, but know I'll also do it because my brother loves her. I think my brother could be very good for her."

It was as ringing an endorsement as he could get. His brother thought this relationship could work.

Jared reached for the mask. He would start the evening off with the truth and pray things went his way.

* * * *

Sarah liked the costume for the evening. It was incredibly dramatic, with a flowing skirt and a top that barely covered her breasts. The hip scarf she'd been given had a whole bunch of coin thingees on it, and they made tinkling sounds every time she moved. Everything but her eyes was covered with a pretty veil that she had to admit brought out the color.

She didn't want to wear any of this crap since she was only going to walk into the dungeon, explain the situation to Sir, and then walk back out again, but the Taggarts were serious about nothing but fet wear on the dungeon floor, and no one would take a note to her Dom.

Jared was out there and he was alone and something bad had happened. She'd heard Alex telling Eve that a trollish jerk had shown up and said all kinds of bad shit that made Jared walk away.

She knew what he'd been doing. Jared wouldn't want a confrontation in front of their friends, and especially the kiddos. He'd led the guy away and Kai had gone to save him. She should have run after him, too, but Kori had convinced her to let the men handle it.

She couldn't do that anymore. She'd given him some time and space and now she had to talk to him. He'd texted her that he was okay and he'd apologized for having to leave early and not getting those cookies, but she'd known that was bullshit. He'd left because he hadn't wanted that ugliness to invade their nice day.

He should have let Big Tag handle things. And honestly, the kiddos were used to blood. Kala Taggart would likely have helped her dad out.

"Are you sure you want to do this?" Kori hurried behind her as she pushed through the locker room door. "I thought you kind of liked this guy."

She did like Sir, but she couldn't leave Jared out there alone tonight. Kai was here at Sanctum. Who was with Jared? Who was talking him through this and holding his hand? Who was distracting him with hugs and long kisses? Kai wouldn't have done that, but he would have done something. Was she going to do that? "I do like Sir. I do, but Jared's more important."

It had hit her squarely in the chest as she'd stood there and watched him, saw his shoulders slump and then straighten again as though from sheer will. She knew that stance. It was the stance a person took when they had to decide if they would break or stand tall. She'd known in that moment that she wanted to be the one standing beside him.

Could he handle what she needed to tell him? Or should she hold fast and be his friend and watch him one day fall in love with a woman who could give him everything he would need?

Or was she being a little bitch by not telling him what was going on? It wasn't shameful. It wasn't her fault.

Didn't she need things too?

"You really think you can give him a second chance?" Kori stepped in beside her, the bells on her hip scarf jingling.

She didn't know. Did she have to know right this moment? "I want to talk to him, to make sure he's okay. I'll figure out the rest later."

Up ahead she saw Charlotte Taggart about to climb the stairs. It was time they had a talk. She hustled to catch the queen.

"We need to talk about why your pit bull of a husband didn't defend Jared today," she said without preamble. There was no time for small talk.

Charlotte was dressed in harem pants and a beaded top that showed off her pretty phenomenal breasts. Sarah wasn't sure how the woman kept them so perky since she knew damn well she usually had a baby hanging off one. Her eyes widened and then she shook her head. "He didn't understand the situation until Jared hustled out of there. Alex came to let us know what was going on, but by the time he got to us, Jared was gone. I assure you we already know who the guy is. Adam had his name and address within twenty minutes. Ian went out to his place with Kai and according to him the dude peed himself and won't bother Jared again. But honey, you have to know Ian can't scare the shit out of every troll who decides to target Jared. No matter how much he wants to."

"I can make it a fun weekend project." Big Tag slid an arm around his wife's waist and dragged her close. "Hello, my gorgeous concubine. I think this sultan is going to need a little attention tonight." He dropped a kiss on his wife's lips before rubbing his cheek over her hair and breathing in deeply. "And some anal."

Yep, they were definitely goals. "So you took care of it? Because if you didn't, I'm going to."

Big Tag's hands were all over his wife. He wouldn't pretend to be civilized in the club. He would let his possessive caveman freak flag fly high here in Sanctum. He glanced up from where he wasn't even trying to pretend he wasn't smelling his wife's hair. "I got it, Stevens. The boy is safe. And if you happen to find out the email addresses of the other assholes harassing him, send them along. I'll let Adam figure out where they are and Kai and I will pay a visit. I never thought about how good a shrink would be at threatening people. He knew exactly where to slide that knife in. It's been a long time since I was nothing but muscle." He grinned. "Though I've got some really good muscles I'm going to use on

Charlie Concubine here tonight."

Charlotte looked like a woman who was used to having a six-foot five-inch hottie all over her most of the time. "I'll hold you to that, babe. So does this mean you're back with Jared, Sarah? You two looked super cute at the game today."

"Don't mention the game. Lodge cheated," Tag said with a lion's pout. "McNamara hasn't been at The Club since he moved to Colorado."

"Yeah, because Jared's been in Sanctum so many times in the last few years," Charlotte replied. "You got played by the original player."

"I don't see it that way," Tag replied. "Just because Lodge is older doesn't mean he's better. Does he have a movie franchise based on stories Serena stole from his life? I think not."

If she let them, they would start making out, and in the club that could lead to actual sex right in front of her. They were a couple of total exhibitionists, and while she did not mind watching, she had other things to do. "I need to tell my Dom that I can't play tonight. Probably not tomorrow either. I'm sorry, but I need to talk to Jared."

Big Tag stood up straight, focused on something other than his wife's boobs now. "You're leaving the party? Because if you don't dance for your sultan tonight…Charlie, baby, that sounds so douchey. Seriously?"

She turned and stared him down. "Whose birthday is it? Did I sit at your feet and blow you while you watched Marvel movies for your birthday? Did I complain?"

"No, baby. You couldn't. That's why I had you blow me." He frowned. "Fine. I was just saying if Concubine Princess here decided to leave her Sultan Sir alone and sad tonight, he can't chase her down tomorrow. That's the rules of this game."

"She knows what she wants," Kori said, stepping up beside her. "If you'll point out the Dom she's been assigned to, I'll let him know she's heading out."

Tag and Charlotte managed to shake their heads in tandem.

"Nope. She's got to do it," Tag said. "And I want to be there when she tells him she's giving him up for…"

Charlotte elbowed her husband right in his ridiculously cut abs. "For the chance at true love."

She wasn't sure about that. She understood why he'd done what he'd done, but it didn't change the fact that Jared had run again. He always walked out on her when times got tough. He hadn't found a way to stick with her. He hadn't let her try to help.

How could she ask him to help her when he hadn't done the same?

She didn't know what the hell she was going to do, but she knew she had to be with him right now. "Fine, take me to Sir so I can get this over with and find Jared."

Big Tag took his wife's hand. "I think we should definitely do that. We're about to get started. Maybe Sir can find some other concubine to play with tonight. Either way, I think it will be entertaining."

"This isn't entertainment," Kori complained.

"Oh, I disagree, and don't you get hypocritical," Charlotte shot back as she followed her husband up the stairs that led to the main dungeon. "You know damn well we can feel for our sisters and be deeply interested in how their love lives are going. Or our brothers. Should I remind you of Vince and his two mistresses?"

Okay, so she had a point. Her friend Vince was Mistress Jackie's sub, but then Mistress Althea had proven to be very good at ball torture, and for some reason Vince was totally into that. He'd had the two mistresses at each other's throats until they decided they could punish him together. She was pretty sure Vince was never procreating.

Nope. She wasn't going there. She shoved that thought out of her head.

It was suddenly easy to not think about it because the whole dungeon had been transformed into a posh harem. Someone had draped the walls in sheets of silk, and a lush carpet covered the floor. There were scene spaces curved around the center, but she couldn't take her eyes off the main stage and its plush seating areas. The other subs were on one side of the stage, a curtain draped across their space. They lounged on overstuffed pillows or luxurious couches as they waited to be called.

The Doms were on the other side of the gauzy curtain, seated and waiting.

From her vantage she could easily see all of them. It looked like exactly the kind of fantasy night she adored, and she hated to miss it. She wished Jared was here, that he was the one waiting for her instead of Sir. But Jared always ran when the going got tough.

And she was still going to skip her chance with this man for him. Because she couldn't not do it.

She was an idiot.

"You want to make a guess?" Big Tag stood beside her, looking out over the Doms. "I know they're wearing masks, but those come off tomorrow night. I'm wondering if you can even come close to the guy you were with last night. By the way, according to Kai, the two of you are damn near a perfect match. You really want to give that up?"

She looked at the Doms, each hot in their own way. And then she saw him. He was standing, facing her direction, but he wasn't focused on her. He was talking to another Dom.

He was such an idiot. The man had literally spent seven years of his life wearing a mask on TV. Oh, this one was bigger than the little green mask he'd worn on *Dart*, but did he honestly think she wouldn't know that jawline anywhere? She'd watched every flipping episode about two hundred times. She knew exactly what Jared Johns looked like in a mask.

"Is that…" Kori began.

"Hey, no talking," Big Tag interrupted.

"It's Jared." He was here. He might have walked away this afternoon, but he was here tonight, and he'd obviously gone to a lot of trouble to "trick" her into seeing him.

Was she supposed to be mad? He had tried to manipulate her. Not tried really. He *had* manipulated her into seeing him the night before. The idea that he didn't know who she was barely crossed her mind. Kai had put them together. He potentially could not have told either of them, but then Jared hadn't mentioned coming to Sanctum this afternoon. She'd talked about it, but he'd been silent. Nope, this was one big play to get her back.

She could only be mad at that if she didn't truly want him.

"Well, I didn't have high hopes of it working," Big Tag said with a sigh. He stepped in front of her, his blue eyes grave as he looked down. "Do you want me to throw him out? This is your home, Sarah. He's the interloper here. You should know he was very adamant about leaving if you didn't truly want him here."

"Don't tell him I know." She couldn't make herself stop looking at him. She leaned over so she could see around Big Tag's body. He was so beautiful and he was here. Was that all she'd really needed? The acknowledgment that he would work to get her? "I don't know what I want from him."

"Then find out," Charlotte said quietly. "He's put you in a position where you don't have to talk about the future or the past. You can live in the now for a few days. You can pretend there's nothing but what's going on today."

That sounded perfect.

"I'll stay."

All three heads turned her way.

Kori's jaw had dropped. "Isn't this the point where you flip your shit about him tricking you? You need to know I had nothing to do with this. Kai didn't tell me a thing."

"Or I can view it as he worked really hard to get me here and I was a little on the stubborn side, and maybe I should take this chance and see what happens." She knew her bestie hadn't tricked her. Kai had been smart not to tell his wife because Kori wasn't the world's best secret keeper. "I think I want to dance tonight."

"Now that I did not expect," Big Tag said.

It was good to know she could still surprise him.

Chapter Eight

In which our heroine dances…and our hero discovers a magic wand…

Sultry music thudded through the dungeon, the signal that it was time to begin.

Frustration was the only thing that thudded through Jared's system. He hadn't been allowed to go behind the filmy curtains that separated the Doms from the subs and find Sarah. He'd been told he had to wait and that to do anything less would make him a drama llama douche bag, and he didn't want to be that, did he?

He bet Big Tag would walk right through those curtains, find his lady and…do what? Break her heart again? Tell her "hey, I'm a douche canoe liar who forgets what Me Too means and won't take no for an answer."

His stomach knotted because he was afraid this would be his last time with her. If she got pissed—and that would be a reasonable reaction—he would have to walk away. He'd promised Kai.

"Sit down." Big Tag sank onto the largest of the big throne-like chairs. He gestured to the one beside him. "Relax. The key is to act like everything is working out exactly like you planned. Even when you fuck up. Trust me. I've accidently pulled pins on grenades before. You lob it somewhere and act like you meant to blow that shit up."

"It's my life I'm blowing up," Jared complained.

"Nah." Tag waved the thought off. "Your life is a mess already. You're just trying new shit. Nothing shameful about that." He clapped his hands and the room went quiet with the exception of the sensual music. "All right, we're going to get this party started. Now my Charlie is explaining the rules of this game to the lovely concubines and I'm going to give it straight to you sultans. First of all, a piece of advice. When you get married, don't let your wives read that romantic crap because that's why we're here pretending to be sultans. Just keep 'em away from it. Women who read science fiction…well, we'd probably be aliens or some shit. Let's face it, women who read are creative and kinky as fuck, so just marry one and understand you'll be doing some weird shit. Now, tonight the sub you were with last night gets to make the decision on whether to move forward. He or she will be brought out and shown to you and then they will either dance for you or explain sweetly that they've chosen not to move forward. You're then free to take off the mask and go party like you're single again. The other half of the dungeon is open for free play, and the lounge is fully stocked and ready for drinking. If you're sad and don't want to play, Li and Simon are down in the locker room watching soccer, and no I won't call it football. If your partner dances for you, feel free to do any and all of the above, except the soccer part. Do not do that. The sub will realize he or she made a mistake. There are several scenes ready to go once the selections have been made, and there are privacy rooms for the super horny, I-want-to-do-it-with-a-person-in-a-mask crowd. Or you can free-range fuck. I don't care. Just clean up after yourselves."

Charlotte Taggart popped up from behind the curtain. "Seriously? I thought we were doing this in character."

Big Tag shrugged. "Do you doubt this is what I would be like as a sultan, baby?"

She sighed and stepped out. "Nope. But let me show you how good I am at playing the concubine."

She started to dance, her hips moving in time to the music. She was followed by a line of subs each dressed in sexy costumes, every one of them taking the game seriously. It was apparent she'd lined them up so they would end up standing in front of the tops they'd been paired with. Some of the subs had no rhythm at all, but there was still a joy in their movements. This was what he adored about the lifestyle. No one would make fun of the subs who couldn't dance. They would be praised for the energy they put into their offering, for the sheer happiness they were bringing the people around them.

And then he saw her and nothing else mattered. She maneuvered her body with a casual grace, the easy move of a woman comfortable with herself, with her own sensuality. She wore a veil that covered her face, but he would know those eyes anywhere. They sought out his and the warmth he saw there nearly sent him to his knees.

He was lying to her.

She stepped in front of him and her hips swayed.

He started to move, shifting to stand, but Tag's hand came out.

"She knows what she's doing," he said quietly. "Let her."

He sat back. There would be time to ruin it later. For now he let himself look at her, the memories of their time together flashing through his brain. If their lives together had been a film, this would be the montage. It would be the part of the film where the audience sifted through each of the moments that brought them here.

Meeting Sarah, her smile so bright it lit up his world and made him wonder if he'd actually seen color before.

That first brush of her hand against his.

Her laughter as she teased him. His ridiculous attempts to get and keep her attention.

The moment he realized how hard his world would be on her.

The kiss. She'd been so angry with him. He'd tried to explain, but every word damned him more until he didn't give a fuck what the world thought. The only thing that had mattered in that moment was getting his hands on her, making her understand how much he wanted her.

The cops pulling him away, that fear in her eyes. For him? Of him?

And then the long lonely time without her.

It played through his head, the uniqueness of their personal story striking through him.

She was it. She was the one, that mystical part of himself that had been missing all along. He could have gone through his life, found relative happiness and never known a piece of himself was out here in the world, but he'd met her. He'd met her and he would never be whole without this one woman.

She danced for him, her hips swaying, and he wished he'd kissed her the night before. They'd touched each other, hands roaming across skin, connected despite the dark. But he hadn't put his mouth on hers. He hadn't brought their lips together and let their tongues tangle.

The music stopped and she fell to her knees before him. He recognized that the moment was playing out around him, and not every sub was on their knees, but he only had eyes for her.

"Would you play with me tonight, Sir?" Her husky voice went straight to his cock.

He wanted nothing more than to keep it up, to pretend for a little while longer. But he couldn't do it. He loved her and he wasn't going to win her with lies. "Sarah…"

She put a hand on his knee, her eyes pleading up at him. "Sir, I would like to play for the evening. Would you take me upstairs so we can play out a private scene? I would like to be alone with you."

"Sarah, I…"

"Take me upstairs, Jared."

His heart clenched. She knew. She knew and she wanted him.

It was enough for now.

He got to his feet. Beside him Big Tag had pulled his wife onto his lap and had his tongue halfway down her throat. To his right, JT was busy watching Sweetie turn her dance into a twerking session.

He didn't have to ask permission. He didn't have to tell anyone where he was going. He was in control because she'd given him that gift. He leaned over and hauled her up and into his arms.

It was time to take off the mask and be real with the woman he loved.

Jared strode up the stairs, Sarah in his arms. He'd ignored everyone who stared at them. Even his brother. He'd caught the thumbs-up, but hadn't even been tempted to stop for a high-five. Maturity. This must be what it felt like.

Or pure lust mixed with something infinitely soft and warm and safe.

He was going to make love to Sarah. He was going to spend the evening inside her and in the morning, they would leave this place together and he wouldn't be away from her again.

Tonight, he intended to let her know what it meant to be his woman.

He reached the third-floor landing and the dungeon monitor looked up, obviously surprised he had guests so early in the evening. The man didn't hesitate though. He quickly opened the door and ushered them inside one of the big privacy rooms Sanctum offered.

"Let me know if you need anything," he said before shutting the door and closing them inside.

He wouldn't. He was absolutely certain everything he needed was in this room. It would have a closet full of toys to play with, lube, condoms, anything he could want. He'd been in clubs like this across the globe and the great ones always were stocked with everything a Dom could need to play with his sub.

What none of those lush clubs had contained had been her. Sarah. His sub. His love.

He set her on her feet, and for a moment he couldn't do anything but stare down at her. He reached up and eased the veil down, revealing the face he adored, the one that had haunted his dreams from the moment he'd met her. She had the fullest lips, like a bow wrapping up the gift of her body and soul. He couldn't stop himself from reaching up and touching her, letting his hands frame her face.

"I thought you would be angry with me." Out of his peripheral vision, he registered the room. There was a big bed and a nightstand. Off to his left was a door that didn't lead to the hallway, likely the bathroom, and if he knew anything about Taggart it also had a shower or a tub to play in. There was a barn-style door that covered what he suspected was the closet full of toys. All he would have to do was push it aside to find a treasure trove.

Those lips quirked up slightly, in tandem with a single brow rising over her eyes. "Then why did you do it?"

"I thought if I showed you how good it could be, I might get away with it." It was true, but not the whole truth. "I was desperate. I take it Kori told you. I didn't think Kai would tell her, but I understand. She's his wife. It has to be hard keeping secrets from her. Don't be mad at Kai. It was me."

Her hands came up and she ran her fingers along the line of his jaw. "Kori had no idea, and you're a dumbass if you thought I wouldn't know who you were. I came here tonight to explain to Sir that I wasn't moving forward with him because I needed to go find my friend."

God, how stupid had he been? She'd seen through his mask and she was still here with him. If he didn't find his control, he would lose it, and this wasn't the place. This was her club and he wanted to be her Dom.

"On your knees, Princess. That's very fitting, you know. I can imagine you with a crown on your head. Get on your knees and we can have this conversation while I warm you up."

Her eyes widened slightly. "Warm me up?"

There was another outcome he hadn't entertained. "You asked me to bring you up here. Did you do that so you could yell at me in private?"

Her fingers slid under the mask and she pulled it off, tossing it to the bed. "No."

"Did you ask me up here so we could have a long talk?"

Those sensual lips of hers turned up in the sweetest smile. "No, Jared."

His anticipation ramped high, his cock tightening further, but he was okay with that. He didn't want to rush things. They'd waited so long. He wasn't going to throw her on the bed and have his way with her. His way with her was going to be slow and satisfying and incredibly kinky. "Then you asked me to bring you up here because you want me to make love to you. I want that, too, but it's not going to be vanilla. I might have started in the lifestyle so I could understand my brother, but I found myself here. Any relationship with me is going to involve D/s, but you've been in this lifestyle as long as I have so I suspect you're all right with that."

"In the club and the bedroom I am."

He needed to make a few things plain. "I assure you I will not limit our sex life to the club and the bedroom. If you let me, I'll have you anywhere I want, any way I like. I won't be polite about it. I know I'm a laid-back guy and most of the time, I'll let you lead. But to stay as laid back as I am, I need to feed the beast and, baby, my beast wants to eat you up."

Her breath hitched slightly, just enough to let him know he'd gotten to her. "I think I can handle that."

He reached out and sank his hands into her hair, twisting lightly. He needed to figure out what she liked sexually. He knew she was submissive, but he wanted to know her particular tastes. She enjoyed suspension and rope play. She liked a spanking. How far would she want him to take her? He tugged at her hair, forcing her head back, and watched as a shiver went through her. Her eyes dilated slightly.

"*Sir* when we're playing, Sarah." He let his tone go deep.

Her voice was breathy, a confection of pure desire. "Yes, Sir. I won't forget, Sir."

He released her, and through the thin fabric of the bodice she wore he could see her nipples had peaked. She liked having her hair played with and there was so much of it, it was a freaking amusement park he would explore to his heart's content. "Now get on your knees while I figure out how to handle you tonight."

There was the sexiest smile on her face as she dropped down to the floor in a graceful slide. Her knees splayed wide and he was glad he hadn't commanded her to take her clothes off. There was something primal about the clothes she wore, and he got what Charlotte Taggart gained from this kind of play. They could shed their everyday modern personas here. They could peel away the layers of the complex beings they were and get to the root of their personalities. He could be the possessive, obsessive male he was deep down, and she could soften and give to her lover the way her deepest heart desired.

Sultan and beloved concubine.

Only here. In reality they were man and woman, lovers and equals, but here they could explore the depths of their relationship, their sexual selves. "If Kori didn't tell you, how did you know?"

Those gorgeous eyes rolled. "Seriously? You wore a mask for seven years on *Dart*. I'm not supposed to know what you look like in a mask?"

"It's a different kind of mask. That's like saying I wore clothes for years. How could you not recognize me in clothes? This mask covers far more than the one I wore on *Dart,* and I shaved before I came in." He'd tried to be careful. He'd known she hadn't recognized his voice. He thought he would do the same with his face hidden behind the mask.

"You can't hide the line of your jaw or the way your lips look. You have gorgeous lips, and I know the way your cheeks crease when you smile."

She'd studied him the way he'd studied her. He pushed the door to the side and sure enough, there were all the things he would need to play with her, to take care of her.

His first time to really play with her, their first session that would end with them making love.

The beginning of his life.

"Well, from now on, I'll know I can't fool you. But still, I was worried when you found out you would be angry with me. I didn't mean to manipulate you." He had to get a few explanations out of the way.

"Yet you did," she pointed out.

"Not very well, apparently."

Her eyes were steady on him. "I was going to come back here. I was going to dance for Sir tonight. Until I saw you today at the game. I knew we had to resolve things before I tried to move on."

The words stopped him in his tracks. "Move on? Is that what

you're trying to do? You want to move on from me? You're going to have to tell me how to do it because I can't seem to manage. It's been a long time and I haven't had a single relationship since I walked out on you."

Her eyes came up, widening in obvious surprise. "Surely you've dated."

Well, that answered one question he hadn't asked. He'd tiptoed around Sarah's dating life because he didn't want to cause trouble in Kai's marriage. "I haven't. I won't lie. I've played around at my club in Malibu, but I've only topped subs. No sex and no relationships. I've performed scenes that involved BDSM and nothing more. I couldn't get you out of my head, hence the ridiculous mask I wore to try to tempt you back to me."

Had he read the situation wrong? She was kneeling before him, obviously willing to submit, but did she plan to do it as a way to move on from him? To get him out of her system?

That could go wrong for her. He was going to make sure he was the trap she couldn't wriggle out of. It would be a mistake to walk away if she confirmed that she was trying to fuck him out of her system.

He couldn't walk away from her again. Not even if she said that was exactly what she wanted to do.

"I've gone on a couple of dates, but they didn't lead to anything." Her voice had gone soft. "I haven't been able to forget you, either. I still don't think this can work but I would like to spend the next couple of days with you. I have to take a trip starting Monday and it's something I need to do by myself."

He had no intention of letting her run off alone, but he needed to figure a few things out first. She was scared of something and she wasn't willing to talk about it yet. If she would give him the weekend, maybe he could figure it out. "I think this can work, but I won't stop you from doing something you need to do. I wish you would talk to me about it though."

"It's something I have to take care of myself," she said, her eyes back on the floor. "I don't want to talk about it right now. It's a sabbatical and it's not negotiable. If you can't handle me taking a couple of weeks to myself, then we shouldn't go any further, Sir."

Tread lightly. He got the message. "You want to take it slow?"

Her eyes were back on him. "I don't know. I think we've taken it quite slow. I would like to sleep with you. I was wrong to cut off our communications and I'd like to do what we talked about earlier today."

"You want to be friends with me?"

"Friends with benefits," she said wistfully. "How about we're friends when you're not in Dallas, and when you are here we explore a D/s relationship? We could start there."

It wasn't what he wanted, but it might be all she was willing to give him now. He'd broken trust with her. They hadn't been together at the time, but they'd both known there was something between them. "All right, but you should know after I finish up the documentary, I'm going to spend more time in Dallas. I'm thinking about getting a place here since my only family is here."

Her shoulders tightened, but he thought he knew what was going through her head. Maybe she didn't need crazy impact play. Maybe what she needed was her Dom to worship her body, to lavish her with attention and affection until she couldn't do anything but sleep in his arms.

He'd seen exactly the toy to help him with that, to sensitize her skin and remind her who was in charge.

"Take off your clothes, Princess. I've got a magic wand for you."

He opened the case someone had labeled *Do Subs Dream of Electric Sheep?*

It was time to make his play.

Chapter Nine

In which our heroine gets lit up…

Sarah eased out of her clothes, careful not to look Jared's way. "What are you planning?"

"You'll find out." He stepped in front of her and glanced down at her breasts, holding his hand out for the top she'd been wearing. "You're every bit as beautiful as I thought you would be."

"You've seen practically everything." He'd played at Sanctum before. He'd seen her wearing next to nothing. She usually ended up topless at some point in the evening.

"But I've never had you undress for me and me alone. I want you naked in front of me. I want you to offer me every inch of your beauty."

"What about the parts that aren't beautiful?" It wasn't a question she'd meant to ask him. She wanted to be utterly confident in front of him, but somehow he'd slipped under her armor.

"There's not a single part of you that isn't gorgeous to me." He reached out and traced the stretch mark on the side of her right breast.

She'd had them since she was a teen, when, according to her mother, she'd "bloomed" early. Her breasts looked good. They were round and full, but her skin hadn't kept up with all that blooming and she had some places where it showed. No one talked about that. A woman wasn't supposed to get stretch marks unless she had a child, and that was never going to happen. It seemed wrong to have the marks and not the joy.

"Do you mind my scars?" he asked, his fingers tracing gently over her skin.

"Your scars are injuries. That just proves my boobs grew too fast."

Before she could say another thing, he tweaked her nipple, a nasty twist that made her squeal.

"You're perfect and these are perfect. Don't say another bad thing about them."

"I wasn't saying something bad. I like my breasts." But she had been thinking they weren't perfect enough. She wasn't a woman who thought that way often. She liked herself for the most part. But he was past gorgeous, enough to make anyone question themselves.

And yet for all his beauty, it hadn't ensured him a perfect life. That was what she'd learned today. She'd known it, known his history. She'd even watched him on what had to be one of the worst nights of his life, but it hadn't been until she'd seen him today that it had struck her deeply how hard it was to be Jared Johns. The world of the famous had its drawbacks.

"I like your breasts, too. We should make some rules." He was back to gently skimming his fingers over her skin.

"How about I tell you if I don't like something and we can hammer out a contract between us tomorrow?" She didn't want to spend the whole night going over hard and soft limits. She trusted this man with her body.

She simply didn't trust *his* whole future with her. She would be the one to ruin it. But they could maybe have the now. It might not work. It might be like a lot of other things—transient. It could look perfect from a distance but fall apart as they got close.

Was she actually hoping for that to happen? So she never had to tell him why she wouldn't give their relationship a real try?

"I can do that," he said, his head dipping down. "Give me permission to kiss you, to have you. I haven't been able to stop thinking about wrapping myself up in you, surrounding myself. I want you to hold me so tight I forget where you end and I begin."

Her body seemed to soften with every word that came from his mouth. He was close to her, so close that her nipples brushed against the hard planes of his chest. They'd tightened right up, prepping for him to twist and tease them, to suck and play with them. His fingers dragged over her neck and across her shoulders, down his arms, but his lips hovered above hers. "I want you to take me, to break me in the absolute best of ways. I want to shatter and have you hold me together."

She would find a way to hold herself apart later.

This weekend, she intended to be all in. It wasn't right or fair to him. She knew she should tell him what was going on, but she couldn't find the words. If he asked her, she wouldn't do it. She would take the chance and it could cost her everything.

Maybe she could take the chance. Maybe it would be worth it.

"Stay with me," he whispered, his hands tugging on her hair. "Unless you want to stop and talk. I'm willing. My dick is aching and I want nothing more than to lay you out on that bed and spend the rest of the night making you scream out in pleasure, but you are more important to me. You, Sarah. Not the sub. Not the concubine. You."

Sweet words that made her ache inside. Yes, this was why he was so dangerous. "I want to forget everything but you tonight. Everything."

She could see his hesitation. He wanted to force her to talk, and maybe someday she would, but not tonight.

He tugged her hair until her head fell back, granting him access to her neck. She shivered with pure desire. His hands skimmed over her hips and caught in the waist of the skirt she wore, dragging them down. He moved with his hands, lips kissing their way down her body. Even on his knees, he could easily kiss her breasts. He caught a nipple between his lips, giving her the barest edge of his teeth. It made her whole body tense. It didn't matter which way he went. If he bit her, she would shriek and moan and love the ache. If he went the sweet route, she would melt. It was all amazing sensation and she welcomed it.

His eyes were on her, looking up as he made his decision. He slowly licked her nipple as he eased the pants off and left her standing naked in front of him.

He licked her other nipple, cupping them both in his big hands. He seemed fascinated with her breasts, and she let him indulge. She intended to give him anything he wanted sexually. For the first time in forever, she intended to fully sink into her submissive role. While they were in the club, nothing else mattered. There was no future and no past. There was only the here and now, and she wouldn't let anything intrude. They could exist here.

He moved suddenly, getting to his feet as though he couldn't stand another second on his knees. As though the anticipation was almost too much. He leaned over and hauled her up into his arms. He crossed the space between them and the big bed that she happened to know had some interesting functions.

"Are you going to tie me up?" She'd dreamed of this, of being under his tender mercy.

"I think I should. Then you can't run from me. And what I'm about to do to you, well, I should make sure you keep the squirming to a minimum." He grinned down at her as he laid her out on the bed then proved he'd been fully instructed on the features the privacy rooms offered. He reached up and behind the mattress, dragging out the restraints attached to the headboard.

It was a matter of moments and she was fully tied down, her arms and legs forming an X that gave Jared full access to her body while managing to make her comfortable. Everything at Sanctum had cushy settings, allowing for whatever play the top and bottom required. He'd tied her so she couldn't get away, but it wasn't nasty tight.

They could get to nasty tight later. She kind of liked it all.

"Close your eyes."

She did as he asked. "What are you planning?"

He could do anything to her. That was part of the fun— anticipation. Of pleasure. Of pain. She wouldn't know until he told her.

"You'll find out in a second, but first I'm going to look my fill. You're gorgeous like this."

She felt gorgeous when she was spread out and trussed up. It was a peculiar quirk of hers. If it was being done in a nonconsensual way she would fight like hell, but in a loving way, it reminded her that he was in this for more than an orgasm. D/s sex was thoughtful, planned out. She would bet Jared had been thinking about this for months.

She knew she had.

She kept her eyes closed but she sighed as she felt a hand on her body. It started at her throat, caressing her briefly before moving down. This time the hand didn't reach for her breasts. He merely ran down the line of her torso slowly, as though claiming the skin like territory. She sucked in a hard breath when he laid his hand flat on her belly, right above her pussy.

And then it was gone and she had to grit her teeth.

"All in good time, baby. Keep those eyes closed. I want you to think about what I'm going to do. Will it be a nice flogger on your skin? Or will I use a cane? I think I saw a vampire glove. That might be fun."

What was he going to do to her? She kept her eyes closed, her mind filled with the possibilities. It kept her on the edge, not knowing what he would do.

And it took her mind off everything except him.

It was the sound that let her know what he'd found, the crack and fizz of a violet wand being turned on and then the clean smell of ozone.

She shrieked as she felt the sizzle along her leg. She couldn't move, couldn't get away. She was forced to take it. Her skin came to life. Everywhere he touched her the skin seemed to jump and squirm and play. The wand could hurt, but he was making bubbles over her flesh, a frothy feeling like she was a bottle of champagne begging to be uncorked.

"I like this," Jared said, his voice low. "I think I could get addicted to spending my nights doing nothing more than torturing my sweet sub."

The wand crackled and she felt the flare as it hovered over her skin and she couldn't keep her eyes closed. She looked at him. There was the most satisfied look on his face, like he was right where he wanted to be. Lightning flashed through her system before he began to ease the wand down her leg. She squirmed against the ropes that bound her, tugging them tight as he explored her body. He ran the wand down to her toes, tickling her and making her beg, back up the opposite leg and to her torso. All the while he told her how gorgeous she was, how much he wanted her. The words were a warm blanket that covered her. It made it easy to be naked when he was still wearing clothes. She was precious to him, desired and beautiful. She wanted to see herself through his eyes.

"You like this?"

She was breathless as she replied. "It makes me crazy so yes, I love it. I've got a strong masochistic streak. I like testing myself."

He winked down at her and amped the wand up, only a bit, but enough that she gritted her teeth when he touched her with it again. "I'm not the sadist my brother is, but I can definitely enjoy making you squirm. I will want to spend long hours tying you up and turning you into my gorgeous work of art."

She could see how it would go. He would spend the entire evening creating elaborate designs across her body, taking his time with each tie. He would lavish her with attention and then show her off like she was his prize, his artistry. She would sit for as long as he wanted, and that time would be hers. She wouldn't have to think or plan. She could breathe and allow herself to be.

So much of her life was making decisions, planning for a future that might or might not come. Her job was to save lives. Every moment she was in the ER was one where a single mistake could cost someone their life. It was powerful and stifling, and she needed this.

She surrendered to the man and his wand. Her magician. He knew how to make her feel alive and in the moment. He made her toes curl and every cell in her body leap with joy and anticipation.

A throaty moan split the air as he lit up her nipples. The sensation was a wildfire surging through her body. She could feel herself getting wet and knew he wasn't anywhere close to being done with her. He'd sparked across her body, her arms and legs, hands and feet. He touched the wand to her other nipple and she could see the blue lightning that connected her to him. It had been like this since the moment she'd met him, crackling energy between them and some indefinable something that happened to her every time they were in a room together. The air was sweeter, any food she ate with him seeming to have more flavor. He brought colors into her life she'd never seen before. He made this different, too. It wasn't the first time she'd played around with a violet wand. Not even close, but because he was the one holding it, touching her, it felt new again.

She felt new when she was with him.

"Do you know where I'm going with this, baby?" Jared asked, his voice deep and low.

She definitely had a suspicion. He'd tickled her nipples and sparked his way down her torso. He was getting dangerously close to her pussy, but then wasn't that where he'd always been going? Her whole body tightened in anticipation. "Be careful."

It was only a part of the game. She knew he would be exquisitely careful. Still, adrenaline coursed through her, taking over and amping up her desire. It was simply part of the glorious mind fuck.

And it would lead to a fuck fuck.

"I will always be careful with this. This is so beautiful." He laid himself out next to her, letting his head rest against her breasts. His eyes were turned down and he watched as he moved the wand. The glass flat-bottomed head was quiet now, but she knew all it would take was a single flick to light up the most sensitive place on her body. Her pussy. He was talking about her pussy. He was about to play with her pussy.

The glass head brushed over her, but he didn't turn it on. It was a tease, a promise of what was to come.

"Do you know how long I've waited for this?" Jared asked, his voice husky.

"As long as I have."

"Longer. I've been waiting for you since I was old enough to realize life would be so much better with a woman to share it with me. I've been looking for you, wanting you. I was lonely without you."

The water was so deep here, far deeper than she'd planned on. She'd promised herself she would go slow, but she couldn't force herself to stop. She knew they should talk, but she needed more than words now. She needed everything he could give her.

And she needed to tell him the truth. There wasn't a place for lies here. Not even to save herself or him. "I was lonely, too. I'm lonely every day I'm not with you."

"You don't have to be lonely ever again." He eased his body up and pressed his lips to hers.

She could practically feel his satisfaction. Fear fractured her peace. What was she doing? He could get hurt. "Jared, we should…"

He flicked on the wand and held it right over her clitoris.

Her eyes rolled to the back of her head and anything she'd intended to say was gone in a rush of pure sensation. Her muscles jumped and she writhed against the feeling. Her body was confused because it should have felt like hell, but there was heaven in it, too. He moved the wand around her pussy, sending flashes of lightning over her, making her wet and warm and oh so ready for him.

She thought she would scream when he decided to be merciful. The wand flicked off and he moved to get to his feet.

Jared shucked his vest and kicked off his boots. "I can't wait another second. You're so ready for me. I can see how wet you are, how hot you are. That's all for me. That's only ever going to be for me again."

So he would be a possessive Master. She could handle that. Somewhere in the back of her head she knew she was going down the wrong path. This was a weekend fling that might turn into a regular booty call, but that was probably as far as she could take it.

Or he could accept you. Maybe he wants you more than anything else.

She shut that voice in her head down in favor of riding the wave of the present. Now was all that mattered. Now was all they really had. The future would come and they would deal with it, but not here. Not now. Now was her time and only her time.

"Only for you." She wished she was lying. She was fairly certain she wouldn't want another man after tonight. Another reason this was a bad idea, but she was full of them and couldn't make herself fix it. She could only watch as Jared unlaced his leathers and slid them off his perfectly notched hips.

He was a god of a man, muscular and perfect, from his emerald-colored eyes to a body that had been sculpted to display the best masculinity had to offer.

And he was here with her.

His cock was like the rest of him, a thing of incomparable beauty. He stroked himself while he stared down at her. His tongue ran over his full bottom lip and she felt like a decadent dessert he was about to devour down. It was not a bad thing to be.

He moved to the end of the bed and stood for a moment between her legs. He was staring at her, his eyes eating her up like she prayed his mouth was about to. She watched as he crawled on the bed like a predator.

He settled in between her legs and lowered his head down.

She tightened her hold on the ropes that held her. She wouldn't last long. Her body was primed and ready to go off.

A wave of pleasure went through her at the first teasing touch of his tongue. Warm velvet seemed to wrap her up and she forced herself to breathe. He didn't have to hold her down. The ropes did that job nicely, leaving his hands free to roam as he licked and sucked her pussy. She hadn't imagined the room could get warmer, but heat blanketed her. The impulse was there to wrap her legs around his head and force him to fuck her harder, to spear her with his tongue, but he was a liar. He was a big old sadist. He licked and nibbled and took her to the very edge before moving back and leaving her wanting.

It was frustrating and she didn't complain because she knew what would happen. If he was half the mean Dom she thought he was, he would untie her, spank her, and start over again. No. She'd offered him her submission and that meant taking every second of his torture.

"You taste so fucking good. You taste better than I ever imagined, and believe me I spent nights lying awake thinking about this." He breathed her in. "I would think about how good you would smell, how perfect you would taste, how soft you are. I was wrong about all of it. You're so much better."

She drew in a sharp breath when she felt him suckle her clit. His fingers invaded her pussy and he started to fuck her, stretching her and curling up inside, looking for her sweet spot.

The tension wound through her, taking her higher and higher until it finally burst over her, the whole world going soft and sweet in that moment.

Then Jared was on his knees. He had a condom in his hands, rolling it over that big cock of his.

And she knew her night had only just begun.

* * * *

Jared was pretty sure his heart was going to stop. It pounded in his chest. He was so focused on her the rest of the world seemed to fall away.

He'd meant every word he'd said to her. She was far more than he'd imagined. Most experiences a man dreamed of came up short when faced with reality, but not Sarah. She was more. He felt far more than he'd thought he could. He'd been waiting for this.

He stroked his cock and promised himself he wouldn't always wear that thin piece of latex. When he'd made her comfortable with him, they would fuck without condoms because he intended to be the last lover she ever had, and he wasn't going to share her with anyone. That particular kink wasn't ever going to come into play. He would be greedy with her, wanting everything she had to give.

She would be the one thing he would never compromise. She would be his, that secret part of her belonging to him as he would give himself to her.

Her heart was so big, and for years he knew she'd felt alone. Never again. He didn't want her to have another single moment where she didn't feel like someone had her back.

He would be her man. He would take care of her, lavish her with his attention, give her everything she needed. He would prove to her that they were made for each other. One day, he would give her the family she'd longed for, all the kids and dogs she could handle.

He quickly undid the ties at her feet. The need to feel her surrounding him was far too imperative to ignore. He had her hands and feet undone in seconds and then was back at her center, spreading her wide.

"I'm crazy about you, Jared." She said the words as she reached up for him.

"I'm glad because I'm in love with you and have been for a very long time." Before she could pull away from him again, he pressed his cock to the sweetest tasting pussy he'd ever had. Her arms came up around him and he pressed inside.

He breathed in, memorizing the moment, the first time, the last woman. He wouldn't love anyone else. He'd spent a year and a half trying to get interested in someone else, but his soul had met its mate and wouldn't accept anyone else.

He took in everything he felt in that moment—the heat of her body wrapped around him, the glow in her eyes as he started to move, the connection that flowed between them.

It was finally the right time—their time.

"You okay?" He had to make sure she felt the same way.

Her legs wound around his waist. "I'm dying but I think you know that. Don't stop, Jared. Please don't stop."

He wasn't ever going to stop loving her, fucking her, being with her. He flexed his hips and thrust deep.

A sexy moan came from her mouth and he could feel the way her nails bit into his flesh. He would wear those marks proudly.

He leaned over, taking her mouth in a luxurious kiss. Their tongues tangled even as his hips kept up the pace, fucking her deep and hard and true. This was what sex was supposed to be when it was with the right person. It was true joining, and he felt more like himself than he ever had before.

Her silky heat surrounded him, making him forget about anything that had gone wrong before. This was what he should have done in the first place. He'd let insecurity and fear push them apart, but he'd been wrong. She was strong enough to handle anything the world threw at her, and she was definitely more than strong enough to handle him.

He twisted his pelvis, grinding down on her clit. He needed to make her come again because she felt too good. He wouldn't last long. Later he would take his time. He would fuck her for hours, but this first time was a tidal wave threatening to crash over him any second.

He would happily drown in her, but he didn't want to be alone.

He felt the moment her orgasm hit. She tightened around him, calling out his name and sending him over the edge with her.

He fell to the mattress beside her, his whole body flush with afterglow. That's why it was called that. It went way beyond the mere sensations of his body. This had been far more than sex. It had been pure connection. When he'd been inside her, he was more himself than he'd ever been before.

Her arms wrapped around him as he shifted off her.

He could barely hear the sound of the music going on outside in the club. It was more of a thrum than true sound, and his heart seemed to find the beat, blood pulsing in a languid, happy fashion.

"I knew it would be good with you." She whispered the words.

He felt his lips curl up in a satisfied smile. "I think we're good together, baby. I think something like this doesn't happen often and we need to make sure we honor it. I don't want this to be our only time together."

"I don't want that either."

Relief flooded through him and he shifted so he could hold her to his chest. "I'm glad. I know you want to take part of this slow."

"Not this part. I think we should do a whole lot of this. All weekend long."

He could handle that, but he wasn't sure he could let her go for a couple of weeks. "Take me with you. This vacation you're going on, take me with you. We don't need to be apart. We need to spend time together getting to know each other as a couple."

That's what they were now. A couple. He wanted to make that clear to the world, but he was a little worried he needed to make it clear to her first.

"I have plans. I can't change them," she said.

"I'm not asking you to change them. I only want you to include me in them. Look, baby, you don't have to do anything. Just send me the details and I'll take care of it." He still had an assistant, after all. She didn't travel with him the way she would have when he was big-timing it, but she handled his travel needs and she was damn good at it. Whatever Sarah was planning, he would upgrade her trip. If she was going to a spa for some relaxation time, he would make sure she got first-class treatment. "I won't intrude. I'll just be there in case you need me. And I can keep you warm at night."

Getting away with her would be the perfect way to cement their relationship.

She took a deep breath and shifted slightly as though she needed to put some space between them. "I don't know that I can do that with you, Jared. I'm fine with spending the weekend with you, but then I need some time alone after."

She sat up, turning away from him.

What the hell was going on? Moments before she'd been languid in his arms. He'd made her happy. He'd given her what she needed physically, and he couldn't think of what he'd said wrong. Frustration welled. He was always fucking up with this one woman. He could have any other woman in the world eating out of the palm of his hand, but this one always slipped away from him.

"So this was about sex." He should have known. He should have fucking known. All of his life he'd been treated like a prize to be won.

She didn't turn his way but her head was high, her spine straight. "It can only be about sex."

"So I'm good enough for a weekend? You'll go off on this vacation of yours and screw whoever you like and then maybe I'll be good enough for a few days if you come back and you're horny? Is that what you're saying?"

"Yes, Jared. I'm saying that."

She wouldn't even look at him when she was crushing him. That seemed the cruelest cut of all. She was done with him now that he'd serviced her. How many women had treated him like a commodity to be bought and sold? He'd gotten used to it, far too used to it. Men, women, they saw him as nothing but a good body and a pretty face. It was why he wanted out of the game in the first place.

But he hadn't expected it from her.

His heart felt like it had twisted inside his body, an actual pain that nearly sent him to his knees. "You know my aunt whored me out to her friends when I was a kid. Well, eighteen, that is. Kai had gone into the Army and left me with her. She was supposed to take care of things because I was far too stupid to figure out how to handle what little money we had. She told me with a face like mine I could take care of us far better than Kai could. I was jealous and pissed that Kai had left. I wanted to prove myself to him."

"Jared, you don't have to say anything." Finally a crack in her armor. Her voice hadn't been steady.

He was more than happy to exploit that crack with the truth. "What? You don't want to know? I thought you wanted to know everything about me. Was that another lie meant to get me in bed? I was stupid enough to actually think that first woman she sent me with just needed a date. I didn't realize what an escort really was until I found myself in the back of a limo with that woman's hand down my pants. I haven't felt that ashamed of anything until this moment. I thought I would never feel that way again, but you managed it. The crazy thing is you told me what you wanted in the first place. You said you wanted to bag me and tell your friends about it. I hope I was good, Sarah. I hope I make a great story. Hell, you said we could have the rest of the weekend. Why the fuck not since I promise I'm never touching you again after I leave this time. You can find your own family. I'm taking mine back."

Why should she get his brother when the only thing she'd wanted from him was sex?

"I think you should leave now. I won't bother you again. I got what I wanted."

He stopped, a million comebacks going through his head, but his brain was starting to work again. Somewhere through the pain and hurt, he was thinking of her.

This wasn't Sarah. If Sarah had wanted sex and only sex, she would have told him that. His Sarah would have looked him straight in the eyes and explained everything to him. None of this made sense.

This…this was why she'd stopped calling him. This was why she was hiding from him.

"I can't go." He moved to her, not bothering with his clothes. He wasn't going anywhere until he understood what was happening.

He stopped, staring at her because she was crying, tears coursing down her face. His anger fled in a heartbeat. His whole soul softened at the sight of her pain. "Baby, tell me what's wrong. I'm sorry I got angry. You touched a sore spot. Please forgive me. I should have asked the right questions. Tell me what's going on. No matter how bad it is, we can face it together."

She shook her head, her hands fists at her sides as though she was holding in a greater pain.

He couldn't even think of what would make her cry. Had she lied to him? Was she seeing someone? It wouldn't matter as long as she chose him now. He wouldn't hold it against her.

"Baby, are you going to see another man?" It was obvious she was aching inside. He shoved down his jealousy because her pain was far more important. If they needed to, he would call Kai and find a therapist for them. They would get through this. "It's okay. We haven't been together. You didn't do anything wrong. Can you tell me if you're in love with him?"

It made him physically ill, but he had to ask the question. He wouldn't pull any more possessive bullshit on her. Now that he was actually thinking about her and not his own needs, he realized he would do almost anything to make this right.

"There isn't another man." She looked at him, those clear eyes sending a shockwave through him.

"What's wrong? Please tell me. We can fix anything, Sarah. Look, I'm not going to hide behind walls with you. I'm going to be open and honest. I love you. I want to marry you. I want to have a family with you. I dream about seeing you pregnant. I think about how I'll take care of you, how I'll rub your feet and hold you while we wait for our baby. I want those things with you."

She'd gone completely white, her face draining of color so quickly he was sure she would faint. But when he reached for her, she pushed his hands away. "Don't touch me."

What had he said? He stood when she did, barely managing to not fall back on his ass. She strode around him and grabbed one of the robes hanging on the closet door, another of Sanctum's small luxuries.

"Sarah, what's happening?"

She belted the robe and turned. "Nothing is happening between the two of us. I thought I could handle it, but I can't. I'm not going on some vacation. I'm going to have surgery and at the end of it I won't be able to have those children you want. So I need you to walk away from me now."

The bottom dropped out of his stomach. "What are you talking about? What's happened? What kind of surgery?"

His head was reeling. She was sick? She hadn't told anyone because Kori would know if she had. Kori wouldn't have been able to keep it from Kai, and Kai would have told him. Kai wouldn't have kept Sarah's illness from him. He knew his brother. He trusted Kai implicitly. So Sarah hadn't said a word that something dangerous was happening to her, that something was happening to her body.

"It doesn't matter," she said, that righteous anger of hers seeming to vanish. "I need you to promise me you won't tell anyone."

He found there were things he couldn't give her. "No. Tell me about the surgery. What's happening? You seem fine. Why on earth would you keep this secret?"

"Maybe because I don't want everyone looking at me the way you're looking at me right now. I don't need anyone's pity."

"I don't pity you. I don't understand enough to pity anyone but me right now." He gripped her wrist, trying not to hurt her, but utterly unwilling to let her go. "Talk to me. Now."

"It was the damn DNA test. That's what did it. That stupid DNA test we both took. I opted for the one that included health information. My mom died of ovarian cancer and I thought it might be smart to just see if I had the gene. I tested positive. I saw a genetic counselor and an OB-GYN. They believe a proactive hysterectomy is the best course of action given that I have a strong history of cancer in my family line, so it stops with me. No kids. I'm not passing this on to a daughter who can hope for a life and get this shitty news. I lost my mom to this. I won't force another kid to go through that. I'm not going to be a wife and mother. There's a chance they get in there and I've already got cancer. I'm going to pray I'm alive next year, and that's all I can handle right now, so let me go."

"This is why you walked away from me?"

She proved she'd taken a self-defense class or two when she twisted her wrist and broke his hold. "I am not going to be your sweet wife and the mother to your two-point-five perfect children. I don't get that life. Now you know. Let me go. I'm saying my safe word, Jared."

He shook his head. "No. We're not playing right now, and you don't get to fucking safe word out on me. This is a serious discussion."

She managed to get to the door and threw it open. "I'm leaving. Don't follow me."

Did she think he wouldn't follow because he didn't have pants on? He did not give a shit.

He started after her, but that was when she played her trump card.

"Deke, I've requested that Master Jared not follow me. I'm using my safe word. Red," she said quietly.

The man named Deke sighed as he looked over. "You need to stay where you are. Should I call Ian? Did he do something wrong? Do we need to have a meeting?"

He wasn't getting kicked out of here because she was being a coward. "She's safe wording on me because she just told me there's a high possibility that she'll get cancer so she's having a hysterectomy and she doesn't want anyone to know. Apparently she doesn't want to be surrounded by people who love her. She's acting like...I don't even know what to call it."

Her eyes had gone wide. "How could you tell him?"

Anger warred with flat-out terror in his gut. "Because you don't get to walk out on me like this. You don't get to be a scared little girl and a stubborn-ass woman all at once. You can walk away now, but don't you think for a second we're done with this. You've got me in a corner, but I won't stay there for long."

"I told you, Jared. I told you why. Leave me be. I can't give you what you want."

"I've learned in life we don't always get what we want, Princess, but I am a man who will fight like hell for what I need and that's you."

She turned and ran like the coward she was.

But it wouldn't make a difference. Not one bit of difference.

He turned and slammed the door between them, then sat on the bed where he'd briefly been happy.

He didn't get up again for a long time.

Chapter Ten

In which walls are torn down and women form plans... and the guys act like guys...

"Did you honestly believe you could hide this from me?"

She thought seriously about not opening the door. Kori stood outside the front door and it was bolted from the inside, so she couldn't simply use her key to invade. But then Sarah realized if she could hear her bestie loud and clear then everyone else on the floor probably could, too.

Why hadn't she bought Kori's place when she'd had the chance? Kori had sold her little house when she and Kai had gotten married, but even the two-bedroom house had seemed too big for her at the time. She was only one person, after all, and she likely wouldn't ever live with anyone else.

So she'd moved into her tiny apartment with thin walls and nosy neighbors who did not mind calling the authorities.

She should have known Jared would rat her out. He was angry with her.

Or he felt sorry for her. She noted he hadn't called her during the night. There had been no pleading texts or messages from him. He'd gone silent and that was good.

But it was obvious Kori wasn't about to be silent.

She pounded on the door. "Do you want to have this conversation here? I'll do it. Let's start by talking about your ovaries."

She unbolted the door as fast as she could because Kori meant it. She would talk about ovaries and cervixes and anything she wanted to as loud as she liked. Kori had no fucks to give, but Sarah had to live here.

"Come in."

Kori stared at her for a moment. "Seriously? It's eight o'clock in the morning and you already have on full makeup and perfectly done hair?"

Of course. She wasn't an animal. She didn't have a problem with those who took less care with their appearance, but it was important to her. It was soothing to put on makeup, and the full-length silk leopard-print gown with matching robe and kitten heels with faux fur were nothing more than her normal Saturday morning outfit.

She'd forced herself to do her makeup this morning because she'd thought it might be Jared she wouldn't answer the door for. She'd half expected him to storm her gates last night, promising her none of it mattered and that he loved her for her.

He seemed to have figured out that she wasn't a good bet, but then she'd known it. She simply hadn't wanted for him to know it.

Kori's hair was flying out in every direction and she wore a Sanctum T-shirt and what looked like pajama bottoms and flip-flops. Gideon and Lahki—who Kori referred to as her asshole chihuahua—were wagging their tails as Kori strode into the apartment.

She shut the door behind them. This was inevitable. She would have had to explain to Kori at some point in time why she had new scars. She wouldn't be able to hide them at the club, and if she didn't go back to Sanctum, there would be far more questions from her best friend.

How would she ever go back to Sanctum now that everyone would know? Maybe he'd only told Kori and Kai.

Well, and the dungeon monitor. Maybe he hadn't said anything. The McKay-Taggart crew could be tight-lipped when they wanted to, even though their leader was the worst gossip of them all. He might view it as distasteful emotion and never mention it again.

This could still work. "I'm sorry I didn't tell you, but I want this to be private."

"You're having major surgery and it's private? I call complete bullshit. I had an ingrown toenail and you insisted on going to the salon with me to make sure they properly took care of it."

She shrugged. "Infections are real things."

"So is fucking cancer."

Well, she wasn't sure what to say to that. "I didn't want you to worry. It might not be a problem at all. This is a proactive surgery. I'm having it done so I don't have problems in the future."

Kori stared and shook her head. "No. You don't get to play that way. You don't get to tell me you didn't want me to worry. It's my fucking job to worry. I don't even understand this. Are we not the friends I thought we were? I sat up all night talking to Kai. I don't understand."

This was something else she'd wanted to avoid. Kai would shrink her to death over this. He would want to talk about feelings, and she wasn't ready for that. She didn't want to have any feelings about this. It was what it was, and there wasn't anything she could do about it. She was numb and had been since that moment she'd realized her ideas about having a family were over before they'd even begun. She was barely thirty and she was going to go into menopause.

Damn Jared for making her think about this. She'd been detached and it had been a comfortable place to be. As comfortable as she was going to be. Now she had to think about it and talk about it. She'd had a damn plan and Jared had screwed her over.

Kori let the dogs off their leashes and Gideon and Lahki started their routine sniff of all the things. It was a ritual she usually found amusing, but now she couldn't focus on anything but the fact that everyone was going to know.

They would know she wasn't whole. God, even thinking the words made her angry with herself. She knew this didn't make her less of a woman. She was a nurse who'd had this talk with so many people. Losing a piece of yourself didn't make you less, but now it was happening to her and she couldn't quite make herself believe it.

It was precisely why she wanted time without the pity she knew she'd get from the people around her.

Kori sighed and stared at her. "I don't know how I'm supposed to deal with this."

"Didn't Kai tell you?" Sarah moved to the coffee maker. They would need some if they were going to hash this out, if she was going to make it through without breaking down completely.

"He has no idea how to handle this. He loves you. Sometimes he's just a man, you know. Sometimes he's blindsided, too. I know I should be all about taking care of you right now, but you don't seem to want that so I'm left with the aching idea that we're not the friends I believed we were. I thought we were sisters."

"I don't want to break down, okay?" Had she been wrong to leave Kori out of it? Kori had an actual sister and a mom. Her sister was a piling heap of garbage human, but her mom was awesome. More than once, she'd thought about calling Kori's mom to ask her advice, but then she'd realized there wasn't any advice to be given. She was taking the only path she could.

Or she could maybe hope for the best. She could be brave and try to have what she wanted. She hadn't even thought about it until that moment Jared had knelt in front of her and said words she never thought she'd want to hear.

I dream about seeing you pregnant. I think about how I'll take care of you, how I'll rub your feet and hold you while we wait for our baby.

What if she waited? What if she gave them a chance?

She shook her head. Any child she had would likely be in the same place she was in. She'd struck out in the genetic department and she wasn't going to pass it on. She knew other women might make different choices, and she respected the hell out of them for it, but she'd made hers.

She'd made it and she'd been okay with it, and then Jared had to walk back into her life and now Kori was here and it didn't seem as cut and dried as it had before.

Kori shook her head as she stood in front of Sarah. "I am trying my best to figure out if you kept this from me because you don't remember how family works or because you thought we wouldn't want to be bothered. I don't give a shit that we don't share an ounce of blood. You are my sister. I will always be here for you even if being here means yelling at you when you're sick because you didn't give me the option of being kind. It doesn't matter what options you give me, I'll still be here and so will Kai."

She flicked the switch to turn the coffeepot on. "I know that. It was never about that."

"Then what was it about?"

She didn't want to have this conversation and she finally realized why. She'd been avoiding this in her head. "I told you. I didn't want to bug anyone about it."

"That can't possibly be the reason," Kori insisted.

"I didn't want you to tell Jared. I knew if he found out that he would show up to save the day, and I don't need to be saved. I'm too busy saving myself." That's what she was doing. She was making the decision to save herself. She knew Jared. He would have immediately shown up with flowers and promises. It was part of his nature.

"I wouldn't have told him if you asked me not to."

"But you would have told Kai."

"I would have," Kori agreed. "I wouldn't have been able to get through something like this without him, but if I'd asked him to, he would have kept it secret, too. God, Sarah, you can't expect the rest of us not to care about this. I don't understand."

Anger flared through her. Irrational rage was suddenly a wildfire in her system. "I didn't tell you because you never wanted kids. I didn't tell you because you would have laughed it off and told me to get a couple of dogs and they would be better companions anyway."

Kori's face went white and tears shone in her eyes. "I would never have said that to you."

"You joke about it constantly." Her hands were shaking.

Kori took a deep breath and seemed to steady herself. "I made the choice and I have to face it every day. I face it from every single person in the world who thinks they should have some say in how my husband and I choose to live our lives and express our love. Do you know how many people ask me when we're having kids? Like every single one of them. When I tell them we're not they smile smugly and say I'll change my mind. I never wanted kids. I'm not wired that way. Does that make me less a woman? Because there are a whole bunch of people out there who tell me it does. I joke about it because if I don't I'll choke out the next person who tells me I can't live a complete life without procreating. But Sarah, I always thought you would. Kai and I have joked about how much we would spoil any babies you had with Jared. Do not think for one second I would mock your pain. I feel it." She touched her chest. "I feel it with you. I feel it for me because I wanted so much to see another Sarah in this world. I wanted that for my sister. I wanted that for my brother-in-law. God, I wanted that for me."

Something broke inside her, some wall cracking at the sight of her friend's tears. All these weeks she'd been a rock. She'd told herself it was for the best. She'd told herself she'd never really wanted kids anyway and that she was happy with her life. How odd it was to want something so badly only when it was no longer a possibility.

Tears slipped from her eyes. "I wanted it. I wanted kids. I told myself I didn't, but deep down I always thought I would get married and have a family."

"You have a family," Kori insisted through her tears. "It's weird, but it's real."

She looked down and Lahki was staring up at her, her doggie eyes wide and filled with sympathy. The pup couldn't possibly know what she was feeling, why tears were streaming down her face, but it didn't matter to her. The only thing that mattered to Lahki was someone she cared about was hurting and she wanted to help.

And wasn't that the most human thing of all?

She got to her knees and held the dog close, letting her tears flow. She hadn't cried once, not even when she'd opened that envelope and seen the results. Not when she'd sat in the doctor's office and looked at the statistics. Not when she'd made the decision to have surgery.

But she cried now. She cried because she'd finally opened herself up. Open to the possibilities she'd lost. Open to the idea that she didn't have to go through this alone simply because she'd lost her parents. Open to the idea that this didn't have to be her whole life. She could survive. She could find a way to have a life.

All the things she'd said to those patients were true. A womb didn't make a woman. Children weren't the ultimate essential to every happy ending. There were choices to be made and paths to be found when those choices were taken out of her hands. The world didn't guarantee her anything—not even a chance sometimes. But she did have a choice in how she faced the bad things that happened.

She could face it with her friends. Her family, the ones she shared blood with, they were gone and they wouldn't come back. There would be no more Thanksgivings where her mom made her special pie or Christmases where her father woke her with hot chocolate. Those days were gone and she realized she'd been mourning them, waiting for a time when she could recreate them.

She couldn't. It wouldn't ever be the same, but she could start anew. She could choose to find new traditions, a new way to celebrate a life that wasn't even close to being over.

Lahki licked her face and Gideon came to help. Kori sank to her knees beside her and reached out.

"It's going to be okay," Kori whispered through her tears. "I won't let you go through this alone. I love you."

They stayed there for a moment, the scent of coffee wafting through the house, something normal to ground her. After a long while, she'd cried until her makeup ran and the dogs were calm again.

There was a knock on the door and Sarah started. "Is that Kai?"

Kori winced. "No. I think I know who it is and I hope you'll forgive me."

She got to her feet, feeling lighter than she had before, though she wasn't free of her sorrow. There was still Jared to think about. "Who is it?"

Kori opened the door. "The sisterhood knows."

Charlotte Taggart stood in the doorway, a covered casserole dish in her hand. "Dumbass. I've known for a while. You could have had this sweet, sweet pancake casserole days ago. Ladies, let's get going. Brunch isn't going to make itself."

Grace Taggart followed her, a brilliant smile on her face. "Sean sent me with very specific instructions for this frittata."

Erin was carrying a big box. "I don't cook, but I can buy donuts. You're hard core, Stevens. I respect that. You almost made it. You got soft and told the man. That was your mistake. You could have avoided all of this. Better luck next time."

Erin was an odd one. "The next time I find out I'm probably going to get cancer?"

Erin nodded as though she totally understood.

"I don't cook either," Serena said, following Erin in. "But I do know the most important part of brunch. Mimosas. Now let's get this party started and get down to business."

"There's business?" She held the door open as every sub at Sanctum seemed to be joining her this morning.

"Of course there is." Charlotte started to turn her little kitchen into a brunch wonderland. "We've got to organize. You're going to be in the hospital for a couple of days, and then you need to be off your feet for a while. You can't expect us to ignore that. You'll need meals and people to check in on you. Kori's going to stay with you when she's not working and when she is, we'll take shifts for the first couple of weeks."

Erin shook her head. "See, you could have avoided this. You could have spent the next couple of weeks in perfect silence."

"And pain," Grace said with a shake of her head. "She would have been alone and in pain."

"Exactly how I like it," Erin retorted. "Now all these bitches will be up in your business and they'll bug you about taking your meds and doing the therapy things. I'm going to have this baby the way God intended—alone in my house, and no one will know she's here until she's two or three."

"You need help," Serena said with a shake of her head.

"She's pathological," Charlotte corrected. "There's no helping her now, and Theo won't let her give birth in solitude, so it'll be okay. And we know she secretly loves the attention."

Sarah stood and stared as her previously quiet apartment erupted in good natured arguments over whether or not Erin liked being fussed over.

"You can't be mad at me for telling your family," Kori said, stepping up to her side. "You might not think they are, but try explaining to the Taggart wives that they aren't supposed to take care of you."

The Taggart wives all had guns. Well, Grace might not be carrying, but she made her point nonetheless.

She reached out for her sister's hand. "What do I do about Jared?"

Kori laced their fingers together. "We sit down and have a lovely brunch and talk it out with some women who might know how to handle a man."

"I know he'll say he loves me, but he wants kids."

"And he can have them," Kori said. "You can have them. Maybe not the way you planned, but we'll figure it out. Together."

She took a deep breath because she didn't have to do this alone.

She had her sisters.

* * * *

Jared glanced at the clock. Another few hours and he would see her again. He'd given her the night to cool off. He hadn't wanted to, but Kai had talked him into it. Hell, he'd spent a good portion of the night talking Kai down. If Sarah worried she was an annoying third wheel in that relationship, she wouldn't have if she'd seen how freaked his brother had been.

He turned his gaze back to the big TV monitor that dominated the Man Cave in Sanctum's men's locker room. A college football game was already playing, but he couldn't have said who the teams were. It was on so he had something to stare at while he stewed.

And waited.

The doors came open and his brother walked in, carrying a big box of what was probably donuts. He wasn't alone. It looked like most of McKay-Taggart was spending the day in the cave.

It was good because he needed to talk to the big guy. He probably didn't have any right to screw up everyone else's plans for the evening, but he was going to ask anyway.

"Hey, how you holding up?" Kai asked.

"I'm fine." As fine as he could be when the woman he loved was having life-altering surgery in a few days. He'd spent much of the previous evening studying everything he could about ovarian cancer. Though it made him sick that she would be in pain, he also kind of wished the surgery was today because he wanted that time bomb out of her body. Like now.

"Some of the ladies are having brunch with Sarah this morning so the guys thought we would hang with you," Kai explained.

"And watch football," Big Tag corrected. "The ladies are brunching and very likely plotting and planning, but we're guys and we're going to watch football."

"Unless Jared wants to talk about his feelings." Kai sent Tag a look like they'd already discussed this topic. "Adam and Jake's wife had a similar procedure, though for different reasons."

"Serena's good," Jake offered. "Sarah'll be good, too."

"That's all you've got?" Adam asked before turning to Jared. "It's complex. I would be more than willing to talk about it, man."

"I don't need to talk about it." He really didn't. He was good.

Big Tag dropped down into the recliner next to Jared's. "Seriously? Is this because you're not going to pursue a relationship with her? Because she can't have kids?"

"Of course not," he shot back. "I love her. I don't give a crap about anything right now except getting her through this and healthy on the other side. I don't need to talk about my feelings because I know what I'm going to do about them."

Tag's lips curled up. "And what's that?"

"First I'm going to take over your club, and then I'm going to trick her into coming and I'll do exactly what I planned to do tonight. I'm going to chase her down, tie her up, and fuck her until she knows who her Master is." He thought it was a good plan.

"Boys, we're playing at the house tonight. Make arrangements." Big Tag sat back, looking utterly content. "You're my favorite, Johns. Now let's watch this game."

Kai shook his head but offered him a donut. "You always surprise me, brother. The set is already built and ready to be put together if you want the whole experience."

"Absolutely." He wasn't holding anything back.

Kai nodded. "I'll help you get everything ready."

Jared took one of the chocolates and sat back.

It was good to have company. He settled in and though he watched the game, his mind was on one thing—her. After tonight, they wouldn't be apart again.

Chapter Eleven

In which our heroine is chased by the big bad wolf and he takes a bite…

Sarah walked into Sanctum with a hole in her heart. It had been lovely to spend the morning with the ladies and she was so grateful to have them in her life. But she already missed Jared.

She was going to have to talk to him. That was what had come out of today's long session with the women of Sanctum. Most of the women believed he would want to stand by her, but she couldn't let him do that. He needed time to think about what it would mean. Although he hadn't called, so it might be a moot point anyway.

She turned toward the door where Kori stood. "I won't be long. I don't have much in the locker anyway. When did Big Tag decide to remodel?"

It had been a bit of a shock when Charlotte had announced that the women's locker room was getting a redesign and everyone needed to clear out their lockers before the weekend was over. It seemed a little sudden, but then they were the king and queen, and they could be a bit capricious at times. If they wanted to give the old locker room an upgrade, who was she to argue? But she was going into the hospital on Monday, so she had to get her stuff out now.

Kori shrugged. "You know Big Tag. He works in mysterious ways. I'll be over at the office. Come by when you're done and we'll call Jared."

She frowned. "I don't know that I should."

"I thought we settled this. You have to talk to him."

"He hasn't called. He hasn't texted. I think maybe he got the message last night. I will absolutely talk to him at some point, if only to apologize. I shouldn't have told him that way and I shouldn't have led him on. I should have laid the cards out and given him time to think about it."

A brow rose above Kori's eyes. "Think about whether he wanted to stay with you?"

"It's a lot," she replied. "The man wants a family and I can't give him a natural one. He wants a kid who looks like him. I get that. He's got some good genes to pass on."

"He's not as shallow as you think."

"I don't think he's shallow at all," Sarah argued. "There's nothing wrong with wanting a child who looks like you."

Kori shook her head. "Ever heard of surrogacy? There are a lot of ways to make a family. Get creative, girl."

She hadn't even thought about surrogacy. Or adoption. All she'd thought about was the fact that she couldn't be the one to carry his baby. There were options. But she couldn't let him make reckless decisions. "He needs to think about it. Maybe once the surgery is over and I've recovered we can try to be friends again."

Kori sighed. "We'll talk about that, too. I'm going to meet Kai. He said he needs to talk to me. I'll see you in a few."

The door closed behind Kori and Sarah took a deep breath. She knew her friend was beyond frustrated with her, but she wasn't sure what else she should do. Jared hadn't reached out. If he'd wanted to talk, he would have been on her doorstep this morning. He needed time and she intended to give it to him.

And if he decided he needed someone else, she would accept that, too. She wasn't sure how, but she would. Wasn't she supposed to want what was best for the man she loved?

She heard the snick of a lock sliding into place and turned, her heart racing just a bit.

Jared stood where Kori had seconds before. He was tall and delicious in all black, from his dark denims to his sneakers to the muscle shirt that showed off years of hard work. He was so lickable it was hard sometimes to remember that the best part of the man was his kind heart. Though he didn't look kind now. He looked irritated. Super hot. But irritated.

"Where did you come from? Did Kori let you in?" Were they going to talk about this here? She'd expected a phone call. It was going to hurt to do this in person.

"I've been here the whole day, Princess."

He stepped away from the locked door and loomed over her. There was a darkness around her normally sunny guy that probably should have had her backing up. She'd never been that smart. Nope. The tight line of his jaw, the way his muscles were tense like he was a predator about to pounce—it simply made her go soft.

But she couldn't go soft now. She didn't want Jared's sympathy. She was truly happy the whole situation had come out and she didn't have to lie about it anymore, but she had to hold the line where it came to Jared. They would both be miserable if they didn't slow things down. "I'm sorry about how I told you. I shouldn't have dropped that in your lap."

"Is that how you're going to play it?" His voice had gone low. Now she could recognize it for what it was—his Dom voice. It was the one he'd used when he'd been Sir. He apparently didn't respect personal space when he used this voice because he was standing mere inches away from her, so close she could practically feel how hot his skin was.

"What do you mean by *play*? I'm not trying to play anything." She hadn't meant those words to come out so breathy and submissive, but he was pushing her every button when it came to that part of her personality.

"Oh, you've been playing with me for a very long time, and it stops today."

"Jared, I…"

"No, you're going to listen," he commanded. "You're going to answer the questions I ask, but for the most part you're going to shut that sweet mouth of yours and listen to me. Every time you disobey means another ten I'll give you at the end of this."

"End of what?" She wasn't sure what was happening.

"That's the first ten. At the end of this scene we've been playing out for the last few years. I sat up most of last night trying to figure out where I'd gone wrong and I realized I went wrong the moment I didn't slap a collar around your neck about two minutes after I met you. I was in a bad place, but I should have been braver because I knew even then that you were the woman I'd been looking for my whole life."

"I know we need to talk. Let's go get a cup of coffee." Anything would be better than talking about this in the very place where he'd made love to her for the first time.

He nodded. "That's twenty and yes, I'm sure you would love to go somewhere civilized where I would have to play the gentleman and listen to the crap that's going to spew from your mouth."

"Crap?"

"Thirty. And yes, crap. Let me make this easy on you. I can make your argument right now. You think I need time to come to terms with the fact that you won't be able to carry my child and I said I wanted one. You fully believe that I can't be happy if I don't procreate, and do it in a wholly traditional way, so you've pushed me aside. Now think for a second because you're up to thirty, and even your masochistic ass is going to be aching because this is not going to be an erotic spanking."

This was the moment when she explained to him there wouldn't be a spanking at all. They didn't have a contract. They didn't really have a relationship. She was going to tell him those things, except she didn't. She stood there looking up at his gorgeous face, completely unable to remember the reasons she thought this couldn't work.

"Excellent." His pleasure at her compliance was palpable. "Am I wrong about what you intend to tell me?"

She shook her head. "No. I think it would be best if you took some time to let this sink in. The consequences are real."

He nodded as though he'd expected that reply. "All right. I think we need to work this out. I'm going to give you a head start. You'll have the time it takes me to get to the control room and set the lights. Any clothing you want to keep, you should probably remove."

"What are you talking about?"

Those stark green eyes of his heated up. "It's Saturday, Sarah. You danced for me last night. Today is the day I get to chase my sweet sub down and make her mine. It's my day to choose. Unless you plan to use your safe word in an utterly cowardly way, as you did last night."

"Cowardly?" He was getting under her skin, but then he kind of lived there since the day she'd met him.

"That's forty," he shot back. "And yes, it was cowardly. You used that safe word like a leash you had around my neck. It is not meant to stop uncomfortable conversations that have nothing at all to do with D/s. It's not meant to shove me in a corner until you want to deal with me again, and if you ever use it that way again, we're going to have a problem. I've already put a clause in our contract."

She wanted to argue about that, but she was up to forty. Forty she didn't have to take because this scene he wanted to play out wasn't happening. Was it?

"You can speak."

Though it rankled, she still responded. "What contract?"

He took a step back. "The one you're going to sign after I've caught you, disciplined you, and fucked you until you can't see straight. Then we're going to get on a plane, go to Las Vegas, and get married. I'll have you back in plenty of time to make your Monday morning surgery, but I will not allow you to go into this without legal paperwork allowing me to make decisions in case something goes wrong. I will be in charge of taking care of you."

This was exactly what she'd been trying to avoid. She knew he'd react this way. "We can't get married because I could die."

"We're not getting married because you could die. We're getting married because I can't stand to spend another day on this earth without being your husband. Now are you going to be a little coward who I have to chase down in the real world, or are you going to be the queen I know you are and make me chase you down here where we're going to find so much joy and pleasure? I can't keep you here. If you walk out that door, it won't be over. I'll still be there for you through every minute of what's to come, but my heart will ache because I'll know you didn't trust me. It's your choice."

He was the one putting her in a corner now. "No one gives you enough credit for being a manipulative bastard."

He shrugged, his muscular shoulders moving up and down with negligent grace. "It's the face, my love. No one sees much past this face of mine, but you will. You have one minute to decide."

He couldn't expect her to decide now. "I need more time."

His hands found lean hips and he stared at her. "And yet you only have one minute. Do we hash this out like the D/s couple we want to be?"

They shouldn't be a couple at all.

But if she wanted any shot at him after this was over, she couldn't walk away. She had to make him understand.

The truth of the matter was, she didn't even want to walk away. She wanted him. If this was the last time they had together, she wanted it. He knew how she felt about the situation. "This doesn't change anything."

"Oh, I think it's going to change everything, my love, but if you still feel the same at the end of this, I'll step back. Not from you. You should understand that unless you get a restraining order, I'll be with you at the hospital and I'll visit you every day. I'll be everything you need."

She turned and watched him start to walk away. "Then what are you stepping back from?"

He turned and the most decadent grin curled his lips up. "From eating your pussy the first minute I can. From proving to you that you don't have to have a uterus for me to make you come like you've never come before. So you'll get all the mother hen and none of the cock. Think about that."

She stood there and watched him walk away. What was she going to do? She wasn't going to get a restraining order. It would hurt Kai if she kept his brother away. Hell, it seemed like it would hurt Jared, and she didn't want to do that.

What would she do if he wouldn't take her good advice and give himself some time?

The lights went out. The hallway went dark, but there was an unearthly glow coming from the stairs that led to the second floor of Sanctum.

"Time's up. You should enter the maze." Jared's voice came over the PA that was normally used to pump low, sexy music through the place. "Unless you don't want to challenge me at all, and then your spanking can be over very quickly. Well, as quickly as forty hard smacks to that luscious ass of yours will take. I don't know. I'm not even tired yet. I still have the energy to lube up a nice plug with some ginger. We can start there. Or you could tire me out a bit and force me to chase you through the maze."

Damn him. He knew she wouldn't be able to walk away, and she hated the ginger lube. Asshole. Glorious, gorgeous, devious asshole. He had neatly put her in a corner, and she wasn't willing to do what it took to come out of it.

She could walk away. The door was right there, and maybe she could have done it if she hadn't spent the morning with women who'd managed to make it despite the odds. Erin had lost Theo, and when she'd gotten him back, he hadn't remembered her. Had she given up? Eve had gone through hell and found her way back to Alex on the other side. Charlotte had been apart from Ian for years.

Was she really willing to not even try? No one got everything they wanted out of life. No one. The universe demanded sacrifices, and somehow sorrow balanced with joy in the end.

Was she ignoring her joy?

She let her bag drop to the floor because she really, really hated ginger lube and she'd wasted a whole bunch of seconds thinking. She should stop thinking and start running because Jared didn't tire out easily.

It was a good thing she knew every inch of this club or she might have tripped over her own feet.

"Yes, that's what I want." He chuckled, the sound coming from behind her. "Run, little sub. Don't think you can hide from me. I'm going to catch you. Let's make a bet. If you can get through this maze before I catch you, the spanking's off and we'll do this your way. We'll talk it out."

"And if you catch me?"

"Then it's my way all the way," he promised.

"You can't make me marry you." She had to hold out. It would be a mistake to not give him time.

"I bet I can. You haven't had me at my best. What you got last night was an appetizer. By the end of the evening you'll agree to anything I want just to have one more taste of my cock."

He was probably right, but she couldn't not call him on it. "Arrogant?"

"Surprisingly, not about much," he replied. "But I know what I am good at and this is it. I do a couple of things well, and fucking is at the top of the list. So it's up to you. Let's see how fast you can make it through the maze. You've got a whole minute on me."

"Or you could just walk to the end of the maze and catch me there." She was starting to think he was sneaky.

"I don't have to do that. I'll have you in my arms in less than three minutes."

Blood thrummed through her. She wasn't sure what she wanted—to win or to get caught. She only knew beyond a shadow of a doubt that she wanted to play. She made it to the floor of the dungeon and stopped to stare. Big Tag might complain about the parties Sanctum threw, but damn the man knew how to go all out. There was a whole maze erected on the dungeon floor, a green, high-walled shrub maze. The plants weren't real, but in the dim light the leaves looked shiny and healthy. Flowers were strewn through here and there, giving the whole thing generous swaths of color. Beyond the flowers there were also twinkle lights threaded through, and someone had left the hamster wheel lit. The soft blue light filtered in and gave the whole place a soft, gauzy feeling.

It was a fantasy world and it was all for her.

She took off running, taking the first right-hand turn offered to her.

"Do you honestly think you can get away from me?" Jared's voice floated through the maze, seeming to come from everywhere at once.

Maybe he was right and this was absolutely how they should do this. She'd made a hash out of it the first time, and she wasn't sure a sit-down with a cup of coffee and a talk about her fucked-up life conversation would really work for them. "I think I'm trying to help you out. I'm going to be recovering for a while. Maybe a long time, depending on what they find. We're not a long-term couple, Jared."

She made another right. Wasn't that what she'd heard she should do? In a maze you should always take a right turn? Or was it left?

"I don't care. Do you know what I've learned over the years? That we don't get to schedule our tragedies or our successes. They will happen when they happen, and how we deal with it makes or breaks us. I will not walk away from the woman I love because her struggle came at the wrong time in our relationship. This is what it means to be a couple. Do you not want to be with me because of the crap I get from trolls? Because it's a lot, and you'll get judged the same way I do for as long as I'm in the spotlight."

She stopped, dragging air into her lungs. How big was this sucker? She thought about the dungeon and how big the space was, but the boys had turned it into a twisty-turny puzzle. She wasn't even sure where she was compared to the regular dungeon. She was turned around. "I was willing to walk away with you when you were at the height of this mess. Right after you were arrested, I went to the police station. You wouldn't see me."

"And I was wrong. I was stupid. I was scared that I would hurt you. You should run, love. I'm very close."

She took off again, even though she couldn't see him coming up behind her. Where the hell was he? Despite the fact that she knew he would never hurt her, her heart was pounding in her chest. Maybe she needed a little more cardio.

Her feet thudded along the floor and then she cursed because Big Tag was an asshole and he'd put up a few obstacles. This one was a small fence that crossed the path. She would have to climb over it. She was sure it would also be used at some point to tie up a sub. She hoisted herself over it.

Or maybe it was meant to tire out the poor sub and make it far easier for her Master to chase her down. She wouldn't put it past the Doms.

Jared would likely simply jump over the little fence like it was a hurdle.

He was so fit and full of life, and she was about to be the opposite.

Was that what she was really afraid of? Or was it merely a small part of the horror she faced? She ran, her brain whirling. She was in a maze, in a place she should know so well, but it was fucked up. She'd stood in this space a thousand times, but now it was twisted, and a place that should be safe for her was foreign.

Like her body. Like her life.

She needed out. She ran, forgetting her plan. She simply ran, her lungs burning.

She wasn't sure how, but she made it to the center of the maze and stopped. It was a mini dungeon, set up with a massage table that was fitted for bondage play. A St. Andrew's Cross dominated one "wall" and there was a table displaying a plethora of toys.

This wasn't a game.

"Jared, where are you?" She wasn't sure she could find her way out without him.

"I never left you. Look up."

She turned her head up and there was her man. He was clinging to the lights that normally illuminated the stage. How he'd gotten up there she had no idea, but from his perch, he could likely see the whole of the maze. She'd never had a chance, but then again, that was kind of the point. She wouldn't have a chance to get away from him because he didn't intend to leave her.

"Be sure. This is not going to be pretty."

He eased himself off the sturdy base that held the lights. With nothing but his upper body strength, he curled off his perch and angled himself perfectly. He dropped down and landed on his feet with pure athletic power.

"I don't need it to be pretty. I need it to be real." He stood in front of her, his hands coming out to cup her face. "I need us to be real."

"I could really die. No surgery is without its risks. And we're not sure they won't find cancer. It could already be there."

"Then do not take a second of time away from us. Not a single second." He leaned over and his lips brushed her forehead.

"How do I make you understand?"

He stared down at her. "You think I don't understand? I took care of my mother when she was sick. I watched her die. Do you honestly think I want to go through that again? I don't. It scares me so much I can't even let the thought in or I won't be able to breathe. But I didn't shut her out and I won't walk away from you. I'll fight with you. I'll take care of you. I won't ever give up on you, and if the worst happens, then I'll be grateful for every single moment I had with you, even the worst ones. That's what a marriage is. Not some happy shit that only works when things are at their best. Not some union intended to facilitate procreation. A marriage. Two people who come together because they don't make sense apart, because they each hold a piece of the other's soul."

Tears blurred her vision. "I don't want you to ache for me."

"I don't ache *for* you," he corrected. "I ache without you. There is only one thing you need to consider when it comes to this decision. Do you love me?"

An easy question to answer. "More than I've ever loved anyone in my life."

"Then marry me. Marry me when we don't know what comes next, only that we'll face it together."

"I'm scared."

"Then marry me and we'll be scared together."

It would be his answer to everything—together. She'd thought she was being brave and selfless keeping him at arm's length, but now she realized she'd been afraid of him, too. She'd seen him as a distant dream. If she loved him, really loved him, it wouldn't always be good. It would be work. It would be trouble. It would mean days where he was less than perfect and he needed her to step up.

It would be a life, a real one with a real family because a family didn't have to conform to some picture-perfect ideal. It was made up of the people who loved you, who were there for you, who didn't let you shut them out.

She nodded, unable to speak.

"That was a yes," Jared whispered, leaning over.

She nodded again.

His lips brushed over hers. "And you'll wear my collar."

Her forever Dom. She'd kind of given up on that. "Yes."

His hands shifted to her hips and he dragged her close. "How do you want this to go? I know you're emotional. I can take you back to your place and hold you. I can be so gentle with you."

He would have to be after the surgery. He would have to be careful. Jared would be tender, shoving his beast down in favor of her comfort. But he didn't have to do that tonight. She was beginning to understand him. Women came easily to him, and his relationships had been shallow for the most part. He'd shown himself to her because she'd taken the time to know him, had spent long hours simply talking to him. If they'd started out in bed, their relationship might have gone the same as his others, but their mistakes had worked to their advantage. Jared liked a challenge. He needed it.

She pulled back. "Don't think you've caught me yet, Master."

She turned and ran toward the outer edge of the maze, thrilled by the low growl from Jared. That sensual sound went straight to her pussy. Her feet pounded against the floor. She wasn't going to make it very far, but she would give it everything she had.

He would have to work for it for a change. Because she was worth it.

She turned the corner just in time to see him hoist himself over the wall and land in front of her.

And Ian Taggart said he wasn't a real ninja because he just played one on TV. The man's abilities took her breath away.

"There's nowhere for you to run," Jared said, stalking toward her.

She pivoted and ran back the way she'd come. She took a left instead of a right this time and prayed she'd been quick enough he hadn't seen which way she'd gone. Maybe if she got out of the maze, he wouldn't spank her. Or she could negotiate with him over the non-erotic nature of the whole thing.

Unless he managed to climb up on the ceiling again. She ran down a long section of the maze and turned right into a dead end. Damn it. She'd never been good at mazes, but then she'd also never thought it would be a life skill she would need. She hadn't planned on finding herself in mazes being stalked by a hottie she was going to marry but who also was going to blister her backside.

She turned and there he was, standing at the end of the path, his eyes fastened on her. He looked feral and hungry, every line of his body tense and ready for a fight. Or a fuck.

Just for a second, she was slightly afraid of him. There was a beast inside her normally sweet and funny man, and she'd brought it out in him. She'd brought that deeply primal part of Jared to the surface.

"Baby…"

He shook his head. "No. No more talking. The only words I want to hear out of you are *yes, Jared* or *please fuck me harder, Master.* But we have a few things to deal with before we get to that part."

He reached out, and before she could step back, he had a hand on her, drawing her to him.

She'd pushed him way too far. It was easy to see he'd held a lot of his anger and fear inside and was likely still doing it. This was a way for him to work through his issues.

God, she hoped he didn't use the ginger lube. "Yes, Master."

He leaned and tossed her over his shoulder. The world upended and she was left with a lovely view of his ass as he turned and started back toward the middle of the maze. At least she thought that was probably where he was going. He didn't have the same trouble she'd had. He seemed to know exactly where he was going.

"Did you help set this thing up?"

A hard hand smacked her ass. Pain jarred through her because he wasn't playing around with that tap. "I helped the guys set it up. We did it earlier today. Every Dom in the place knew exactly how to get through the maze. The game was always going to be rigged in our favor. We simply wanted you to believe you had a chance. I was never going to let you get away from me."

He reached the center of the maze and lowered her to the table set up there.

"That doesn't seem fair." Not that she cared now. She didn't want to win this game if it meant not being here with Jared. Some things were worth losing.

Even with her sitting on the table, he loomed over her. His hands came up to brush against her neck. "Nothing about this is fair."

She was pretty sure he wasn't merely talking about the games the Doms intended to play. He was talking about life. He was talking about them.

His hands shifted down and then he was doing something totally unfair. He ripped the blouse she was wearing in two.

"Jared," she said, even as he was pulling the shirt from her and tossing it away.

"I told you if you wanted to save your clothes you should take them off." He turned his attention to the table where the toys lay.

She had to think those were all for her since they were laid out in a specific order. His fingers touched a pretty set of what most people would think were earrings, but she knew were meant for other parts of her body. "You said that and then only gave me a few minutes to run."

She quickly pulled her bra off because it wasn't cheap, and it was surprisingly comfortable.

"You have to make choices in life," he replied. "Get out of the pants now, and then I want your arms behind your back."

There was no give in the man's words. She slid off the table, kicked off her shoes and dragged off her pants and undies before doing exactly as he asked. He needed some control, and it was hers to give him. That was the exchange. Control for pleasure.

At least that was the exchange here. In their normal lives it would be so much more. They would exchange vows. They would give of themselves to try to ensure the other's happiness.

Her days would be better because she shared them with him. No matter how many they had left.

She gripped her wrists behind her back, a position that forced her breasts out.

Jared stood in front of her, staring down at her chest. "Tell me you're mine."

She'd done a number on him. "I'm yours."

She was through fighting. Hadn't she learned that sometimes submitting could be the sweetest thing she could do? Sometimes when she gave in, she got the most out. She was submitting to this man, giving over her heart and trusting him not to break it.

He needed her, too. He needed her to be his safe place.

He fell to his knees and cupped her right breast. She held her breath as he molded her to his hand and then leaned forward to capture her nipple between his lips. Pure arousal shot through her. She felt the tiny sting as he nipped at her, but it only heightened her need. He tongued her, moving back and forth between her breasts. She did her best to stay still, to give him what he wanted. After a few moments' torture, the real fun began as he slipped the jeweled clamp on her right nipple, and then the left. The set was connected with a thin chain that hung below her breasts when he was done. She let the pain sink into her skin as he tightened the clamps. Heat rushed through her and she could feel her body getting soft and warm for him.

He sat back on his heels, staring at his work. He tugged gently on the chain that connected her breasts to each other and seemed satisfied with the way she gasped and squirmed.

"That's better." A single finger ran down the line of her body, from the valley of her breasts over her belly and down to her pussy. "Are you getting wet for me?"

"Yes."

"I have to test it because you've been known to lie."

"I didn't lie, Jared. I just didn't tell you everything."

He slid a single finger over her clitoris, just enough to make her take a deep breath, to let him know how desperate she was starting to get. "I need you to understand that not telling me something incredibly important is tantamount to lying to me, and I won't put up with it."

That finger slid over her pussy, proving how slick she was. Being here with him was making her hot. If he rubbed her for even a few seconds she might be able to start the afternoon right. A spanking would be so much easier to take if she'd recently had an orgasm.

He pulled his hand away, bringing his fingers to his lips. He stared at her as he licked his fingers clean. The man knew exactly how to get to her. Watching him taste her made her think about what he could do when he put his mouth on her pussy and ate his fill.

"You weren't lying about this at least." He pulled a chair to the center of the little space and sat himself down, patting his lap. "Unfortunately, we need to get the punishment portion of this scene over with."

Damn it. She'd hoped he would forget about that part. Still, it wasn't like she didn't enjoy a spanking.

"Put yourself over my lap in ten seconds or I'll double the punishment. You know what your safe word is. You've used it so recently."

Okay, maybe she shouldn't have used it that way. She hurried to lay herself over his lap. The clamps bounced and caused her to hiss at the stinging pain. He'd known exactly what he was doing, and she was deeply grateful she'd managed to avoid the figging he'd threatened her with.

"Count it out for me."

Before she could respond to him, his hand came down on her ass and she had to hold on to his ankles. He hadn't held back and the man worked out. He'd already proven his upper body strength. Did he have to do it again?

"I need a count, Sarah."

Bastard. "One."

He slapped her ass again.

"Two." She gritted her teeth and tried to relax.

"You will never keep something like that from me again." He slapped her ass another five times, pausing to let her count each time.

He didn't wait for her to respond, merely went right back to his work.

She found a rhythm to his torture. Pain and heat, and then it sank into her skin, her muscles giving in and relaxing. Only to start over again. She counted each smack of his hand. He spread them out, peppering her ass with heat and sensation.

Around thirty she sagged against him.

He stopped, his hand smoothing over her skin. It was likely nice and pink.

"I'm okay, Master. Not even thinking about using a safe word." She might never use it again. "You can finish."

This smack jarred her. "I will finish when I decide to finish, brat."

She went still. She wasn't usually this bratty in the middle of a scene. She stroked his leg. He was still on the edge and would be for a while. It was odd how calm she felt about the surgery knowing Jared would be there. His anxiety seemed to have quelled her own.

"You're so beautiful." His fingers brushed against her skin. "Your ass looks good pink, brat. I think it will be that way a lot."

She rubbed her cheek against his leg. "Probably."

"And this didn't bother you at all, did it?" He smacked her ass, a lighter touch this time, as though he was coming down, too.

"No. I enjoyed it. I'm afraid if you're really going to punish me, you'll have to make me sit in a corner and not talk. That would bother me. This mostly makes me want to have wicked sex with you, but I'll be honest, most things do that."

He chuckled, running his hand over her skin. "Is that true? I think I can handle that. And I'm going to hold my last nine strokes for a later date. If I can't truly punish you, then I'll reward myself. Get on your knees, my love."

He shifted her off his lap and she found herself on her knees between his legs, staring at the place where his cock pressed against his jeans.

Oh, yes. She could do that.

* * * *

Jared wasn't sure he would survive this experience. Sarah reached out and gently started to open the fly of his jeans. He wanted to do it himself and then shove her head toward his cock, but he was determined to prove he had some restraint.

He'd never had to prove it before her. He was always in control when it came to sex. Control was a necessary part of the pleasure, but with Sarah sex was a wildfire that threatened to consume them both. He wanted to take his time with her. His sub. His wife.

She was going to be his wife.

God, he couldn't lose her.

"Stay with me." Sarah stared up at him as though she could read his mind. "I want to be alone with you. I don't want it in here."

It. The surgery. The chance that she might have cancer. It threatened to swallow him up, but he had to be stronger than that today. He had to concentrate on her. "Then you should take my mind off it. You should make sure I can't think about anything but the way your mouth feels on my cock. Do you think you can do that?"

She smiled up at him. "I think I can, Master."

She eased the fly of his jeans apart, and he had to take a deep breath when her soft hand brushed his cock. His whole body tightened.

He hadn't scared her at all. He knew he'd been rough on her, but he'd needed to know exactly how she liked to play. And he'd needed her to submit to him today. Tomorrow would be another story. Tomorrow he would get on his knees for her, but today, he needed this.

And that was what their marriage would be like, each gracefully bending to be what the other needed.

What he needed right now was her mouth on his cock. He needed to spend the next couple of days naked against her, curled up beside her when he wasn't inside her.

She took his cock in hand and then he wasn't thinking about the future or the past. There was nothing at all but how she could make him feel.

"Grip me harder."

She tightened that perfectly manicured hand around his cock. Her nails were always some pretty color. He adored that about her. Now he watched as those pink-tipped hands stroked him right before she leaned over and dragged her tongue over the head of his dick.

His eyes nearly rolled to the back of his head. She lavished his cock with affection, playing with him like he was her favorite toy. He knew he should be more in control, but he was far too busy watching her, watching the way his cock disappeared behind her sultry lips, how her tongue curled around him and darted out to lap up the bead of arousal that pulsed from the slit.

All the while her hand stroked him, squeezing him the way her pussy was going to when he got inside her. She would be so tight he wouldn't be able to breathe, wouldn't be able to do anything except pump himself inside her.

He hissed when her teeth scraped lightly over him and he knew he wasn't going to last long. He didn't want to come in her mouth. There would be more than enough time for that later. Later he would come all over her, but this first time since the moment they'd promised to be together, this time he wanted her with him.

He wound his hands in her hair. He fucking loved her hair. He would love waking up tangled in that gorgeous hair. He tugged on it and her gaze drifted up, pure mischief in her eyes.

Such a brat. "Take me deep but stop when I tell you to. Follow my lead."

He controlled her movements with her hair, shoving his cock deep into her mouth while he pulled her close. She gave up stroking him and her hands found his thighs, holding on and giving her balance. If he hadn't left his jeans on, those nails would be sinking into his skin and he would have loved that. He would be proud to wear the marks of her passion, to feel that tiny ache the next day.

She took him deep, enclosing him in soft heat.

It was all he could take. He tugged on her hair and she sat back. She was so stunningly gorgeous with her breasts bejeweled, her nipples like ripe raspberries. Thank god she was a masochist because he had a bit of the sadist in him. He was looking forward to the way she would squirm when he took them off. But first...

He stood in front of her and tugged his shirt over his head. "Take my jeans off."

She reached up and helped tug his jeans down his thighs. Her head brushed against his cock, letting it rub over her cheek. It was a sweet gesture in the middle of sex and a sure sign that he was with the right woman. He needed her affection as much as he did her submission.

"Come up here." He stepped out of his jeans and reached out to help her up. He pulled her body against his, skin to skin. Where he wanted to be always. "I love you. I love you, Sarah Stevens. I want to be with you no matter what happens."

Her hands came up to frame his face. "No matter what."

He kissed her, locking their mouths together even as he reached down and cupped her ass and ground himself against her. He moved her back to the table without ever letting go. He eased her down and spread her legs. She was already wet and ready for him.

He pressed himself against her. "Is this okay?"

Her eyes widened as she realized what he was asking. She nodded solemnly. "It's okay."

He had a condom ready, but there wasn't a need for it. Not now. It was an ache, but one that could be eased because they shared it.

Jared brought them together. Sarah wrapped her arms and legs around him, opening herself body and soul to him.

It was everything he'd wanted. His whole life he'd been looking for a place to belong and it was with this woman, in this time.

He wouldn't let her go. He would never let her go.

He found a rhythm, thrusting in and pulling out. Anticipation coursed through him as the pleasure built. He held out as long as he could, watching her come again and again, but he couldn't hold out forever. When he felt his own orgasm start, he leaned over and kissed her, bringing them as close as they could.

It washed over him, the pleasure, but beyond that the connection he felt to this woman.

It was all he needed.

He held her close as he came down from the high of loving her and promised himself everything would be okay.

Chapter Twelve

In which a family comes together and happily ever afters aren't always perfectly normal...

Sarah held her husband's hand as the doctor walked out the door. Not long now. She was prepped and all they were waiting for was the OR.

The last forty-eight hours played through her brain, a glorious combination of sex and love and ridiculous decadence. Jared had flown them in a private plane to Vegas, where Kori and Kai had been their witnesses as they'd exchanged vows. Then they'd dumped their friends and hadn't left their suite until they'd been forced to come home Sunday afternoon.

Then he'd held her through the night because today was the day.

"Okay. In an hour or two we'll be done," Jared said, squeezing her hand. "And then we should know something."

Then they would know if they'd caught it in time or if she needed chemotherapy, something else they would face together.

"I think it's going to be okay," she said, looking up at him. He hadn't slept all night. He was being strong for her, but she knew how afraid he was. It made her calmer, as though they were working as a team and only one of them could be freaked out at a time. "I think we caught it super early and we're stopping it before it can even begin."

He nodded but she could still see the tension in his eyes.

"Hey, could I have a minute with her?" Kori stood in the doorway.

"They're going to take her in a couple and I have something I need to say."

Jared nodded. "Of course. I'll be outside with...well, I'll be outside."

She let him go and looked at her best friend. Sometimes she wasn't sure she remembered a time when they weren't friends. She knew it existed, but they'd been together for so long that time seemed hazy. Tears pierced her eyes. They'd started out as two subs who were absolutely not looking for love, and somehow they'd become sisters and now sisters-in-law.

"It's going to be okay."

Kori reached for her hand. "It better be or I'm going to fuck some people up." She took a deep breath. "Look, I know it's going to be okay because it has to. It's going to be fine and that's why I want to talk to you about the future."

"Jared's taking a couple of months off and then he's thinking about getting more into the documentary scene," Sarah explained. "He's really liked working on this personal one, but he's been talking to Mia. She's got some ideas but she doesn't have any film experience. I think it could be cool."

"I'm not talking about that," Kori corrected. "Jared is going to be great at anything he puts his mind to and so will you. And I think you would be the best mom in the world, and that's why I want to be your surrogate when you're ready. I've thought a lot about this and we could use my egg and Jared's sperm. Or someone else's egg. I think Charlotte Taggart has like a lot of them from what I can tell. You might want someone taller."

She held on to her friend's hand, utterly floored by the offer. "Kori, you don't want kids."

She nodded her head vigorously. "That's the surrogacy part. You have to take the kid at the end, and you're probably only getting one out of me because I will not like the whole labor thing."

The whole world was a blurry mess. "You don't..."

Her friend stared down at her. "I do because two of the people I love most in this world are going to need a little help and I won't let them down. I want to do this for you. I want it for me too because I can't wait to see how you handle being a mom. I'm going to live stream you dealing with the first poopy diaper."

Laughter bubbled up in her. How had she ever kept this quiet? She needed her family, even if it was small. Even if it was only Jared and Kori waiting for her, she needed them. "And I'll stream the first time that sucker kicks you from the inside."

A brilliant smile crossed Kori's face. "We'll do it together."

Like they'd done everything for the last decade.

The door opened and the nurse walked in. "We're ready for you. And you should know that your husband arranged this with the hospital. That man loves you since he had to bribe them with monthly visits to the kid's wing from all manner of superheroes."

"Arranged what?" Sarah asked as the nurse popped the brakes off her bed.

"Every princess needs a royal court," Kori said with a grin.

She looked down the hallway that would lead her to the elevator to the operating room. The hallway was lined with her friends from the club. They stood on either side, whole families coming out to support her. Ian and Charlotte Taggart were there with their twins, Seth held in his father's arms. The twins stood with some of the other kiddos she babysat once a week in the nursery. She'd watched them grow and now they were standing there with hand-made signs that looked like they'd bought out a glitter store to decorate.

We love you Auntie Sarah!

You got this!

Jared stepped in beside her and took her hand again. "They wanted to be here for you."

Kai was at the front of the line. "We'll be waiting. Not a one of us can work until we know you're okay."

She cried as they pushed her toward the elevator, but it wasn't from fear. It was the overwhelming love she felt. These people she "played" with, who she'd met in a place where they didn't have to be real, turned out to be far more real than she could have imagined.

"You got this," Serena Dean-Miles said as she passed. Serena had been faced with this same surgery before. "I'll see you on the other side and we'll compare notes."

"Don't worry about a thing." Mia was there and Sarah had been almost certain she'd been in New York yesterday.

"Did you fly in?"

Mia smiled. "I wouldn't miss it. Not for the world. Love you, sister."

They said it over and over, each one offering her words of love and encouragement.

Jared walked with her right until the elevator doors opened.

The rest she had to do on her own.

"I'll be here," he whispered, kissing her one last time.

"I love you, babe. See you in a bit."

The doors closed and she was ready.

* * * *

Six Months Later

Jared John Ferguson loved being a husband. Her husband. The first months of their marriage had been the fulfillment of his promise—to take care of her. From the moment he'd learned she was all right, he'd thought of nothing but her comfort. He'd put aside those things he'd thought he'd wanted—the career, the fame, the trappings of a successful life—and in those first few days, helping his wife to the bathroom had been the focus of his world. Making sure she got her medications, that she had what she needed.

He'd done the things he'd promised he would do if she ever got pregnant. It had been foolish to think that would be the only time to do it, when he was waiting on his family. She was already here.

He'd carried her over the threshold of their home because she'd been too weak to carry herself, but she'd gotten stronger. Every day she found she could do more. The surgery had been harder on her because they'd had to open her up. But they'd gotten everything they needed to, and they'd gotten to it in time. No chemotherapy for his love.

His wife would be just fine.

She'd proven to be a great partner. While she'd been recovering, she'd taken to helping him put together the documentary. She'd done her interview when she'd felt well enough and had been his sounding board. Next month they would get to take a trip. To Utah where he would show the documentary at Sundance.

"Are you ready?" Kai asked, bringing him out of his thoughts. "You sure you can make this work? You need some porn or something?"

Those words reminded him he was in the fertility clinic about to do something that would change all their lives.

His brother would never stop teasing him about this. Of course it was sort of real. He'd never thought he would be partially conceiving his son or daughter in a doctor's office. "You should know I've always been able to masturbate."

Kai shuddered. "Yeah, you should have remembered to lock your door more often. I hope this kid is a boy so you have to deal with yourself as a teen."

"Are you really okay with this?" They'd been doing that manly brotherly thing the last couple of weeks since they'd decided to give IVF and surrogacy a try. But this was Kai's wife who was offering to carry his brother's child. It was weird.

And so beautiful it made his heart clench to think about what Kori was offering them.

Kai put a hand on his shoulder. "I've never been prouder of my wife than I was when she told me she wanted to do this. And I'm pretty fucking proud of her all the time. I want this for you, brother. Go and get me and Kori a dumbass nephew or super sweet niece to spoil."

He stood up, the waiting room around him nicely furnished but absolutely not how he'd thought he would be doing this kind of thing.

Was he actually going to be able to do this?

"Mr. Ferguson, the room is ready for you," the nurse said, holding open the door to the waiting room.

He stared at her for a moment. It was surreal. He was going to walk into some room where a whole bunch of guys had masturbated into a cup and do his business and then the nurse was going to take it and he might be a father in less than a year.

It would be so much easier if Sarah had come with him, but she'd had some stuff to finish up with. Or that was the excuse she'd given so Kai had driven him.

Why had he had his brother drive him?

"Jared, it's okay," Kai said. "I want you to go in there and pretend it's just another night at Sanctum and you're doing a medical scene. Do you want to talk about this?"

He practically ran for the nurse because he was not talking about this with his brother. Nope. He strode down the hallway, was given his little cup to make his deposit in, and then he was standing in front of the door.

"If you need anything, let me know," the nurse said with a wink.

He watched her walk away and then pulled his cell phone out. Only one thing would work. He couldn't do this without her. He needed his wife.

Text me a picture of your breasts.

Short. Simple. A command that she wouldn't refuse. His wife was a bit of an exhibitionist, after all. They'd been back at Sanctum long before she'd been cleared for play. They'd simply held each other and watched the scenes and been a part of the fun.

A familiar sound hit his ears. The angelic chiming Sarah used for his texts.

His body went on full alert and he opened the door because he had a feeling he wouldn't have any trouble filling that cup now.

His gorgeous wife was standing in the middle of the room wearing the sexiest naughty nurse costume he'd ever seen. "Hey, babe. Thought you might need some help."

His whole soul warmed when he saw her. "Damn straight. Let's make a baby."

He closed the door behind him and got down to business.

* * * *

Also from 1001 Dark Nights and Lexi Blake, discover Protected, Close Cover, Arranged, Dungeon Games, Adored, and Devoted.

Sign up for the 1001 Dark Nights Newsletter
and be entered to win a Tiffany Key necklace.

There's a contest every month!

Go to www.1001DarkNights.com to subscribe.

**As a bonus, all subscribers can download
FIVE FREE exclusive books!**

Discover 1001 Dark Nights Collection Six

Go to www.1001DarkNights.com for more information.

DRAGON CLAIMED by Donna Grant
A Dark Kings Novella

ASHES TO INK by Carrie Ann Ryan
A Montgomery Ink: Colorado Springs Novella

ENSNARED by Elisabeth Naughton
An Eternal Guardians Novella

EVERMORE by Corinne Michaels
A Salvation Series Novella

VENGEANCE by Rebecca Zanetti
A Dark Protectors/Rebels Novella

ELI'S TRIUMPH by Joanna Wylde
A Reapers MC Novella

CIPHER by Larissa Ione
A Demonica Underworld Novella

RESCUING MACIE by Susan Stoker
A Delta Force Heroes Novella

ENCHANTED by Lexi Blake
A Masters and Mercenaries Novella

TAKE THE BRIDE by Carly Phillips
A Knight Brothers Novella

INDULGE ME by J. Kenner
A Stark Ever After Novella

THE KING by Jennifer L. Armentrout
A Wicked Novella

QUIET MAN by Kristen Ashley
A Dream Man Novella

ABANDON by Rachel Van Dyken
A Seaside Pictures Novella

THE OPEN DOOR by Laurelin Paige
A Found Duet Novella

CLOSER by Kylie Scott
A Stage Dive Novella

SOMETHING JUST LIKE THIS by Jennifer Probst
A Stay Novella

BLOOD NIGHT by Heather Graham
A Krewe of Hunters Novella

TWIST OF FATE by Jill Shalvis
A Heartbreaker Bay Novella

MORE THAN PLEASURE YOU by Shayla Black
A More Than Words Novella

WONDER WITH ME by Kristen Proby
A With Me In Seattle Novella

THE DARKEST ASSASSIN by Gena Showalter
A Lords of the Underworld Novella

Also from 1001 Dark Nights:
DAMIEN by J. Kenner

Discover 1001 Dark Nights

Go to www.1001DarkNights.com for more information.

COLLECTION ONE
FOREVER WICKED by Shayla Black
CRIMSON TWILIGHT by Heather Graham
CAPTURED IN SURRENDER by Liliana Hart
SILENT BITE: A SCANGUARDS WEDDING by Tina Folsom
DUNGEON GAMES by Lexi Blake
AZAGOTH by Larissa Ione
NEED YOU NOW by Lisa Renee Jones
SHOW ME, BABY by Cherise Sinclair
ROPED IN by Lorelei James
TEMPTED BY MIDNIGHT by Lara Adrian
THE FLAME by Christopher Rice
CARESS OF DARKNESS by Julie Kenner

COLLECTION TWO
WICKED WOLF by Carrie Ann Ryan
WHEN IRISH EYES ARE HAUNTING by Heather Graham
EASY WITH YOU by Kristen Proby
MASTER OF FREEDOM by Cherise Sinclair
CARESS OF PLEASURE by Julie Kenner
ADORED by Lexi Blake
HADES by Larissa Ione
RAVAGED by Elisabeth Naughton
DREAM OF YOU by Jennifer L. Armentrout
STRIPPED DOWN by Lorelei James
RAGE/KILLIAN by Alexandra Ivy/Laura Wright
DRAGON KING by Donna Grant
PURE WICKED by Shayla Black
HARD AS STEEL by Laura Kaye
STROKE OF MIDNIGHT by Lara Adrian
ALL HALLOWS EVE by Heather Graham
KISS THE FLAME by Christopher Rice
DARING HER LOVE by Melissa Foster
TEASED by Rebecca Zanetti
THE PROMISE OF SURRENDER by Liliana Hart

COLLECTION THREE
HIDDEN INK by Carrie Ann Ryan
BLOOD ON THE BAYOU by Heather Graham
SEARCHING FOR MINE by Jennifer Probst
DANCE OF DESIRE by Christopher Rice
ROUGH RHYTHM by Tessa Bailey
DEVOTED by Lexi Blake
Z by Larissa Ione
FALLING UNDER YOU by Laurelin Paige
EASY FOR KEEPS by Kristen Proby
UNCHAINED by Elisabeth Naughton
HARD TO SERVE by Laura Kaye
DRAGON FEVER by Donna Grant
KAYDEN/SIMON by Alexandra Ivy/Laura Wright
STRUNG UP by Lorelei James
MIDNIGHT UNTAMED by Lara Adrian
TRICKED by Rebecca Zanetti
DIRTY WICKED by Shayla Black
THE ONLY ONE by Lauren Blakely
SWEET SURRENDER by Liliana Hart

COLLECTION FOUR
ROCK CHICK REAWAKENING by Kristen Ashley
ADORING INK by Carrie Ann Ryan
SWEET RIVALRY by K. Bromberg
SHADE'S LADY by Joanna Wylde
RAZR by Larissa Ione
ARRANGED by Lexi Blake
TANGLED by Rebecca Zanetti
HOLD ME by J. Kenner
SOMEHOW, SOME WAY by Jennifer Probst
TOO CLOSE TO CALL by Tessa Bailey
HUNTED by Elisabeth Naughton
EYES ON YOU by Laura Kaye
BLADE by Alexandra Ivy/Laura Wright
DRAGON BURN by Donna Grant
TRIPPED OUT by Lorelei James
STUD FINDER by Lauren Blakely
MIDNIGHT UNLEASHED by Lara Adrian

HALLOW BE THE HAUNT by Heather Graham
DIRTY FILTHY FIX by Laurelin Paige
THE BED MATE by Kendall Ryan
NIGHT GAMES by CD Reiss
NO RESERVATIONS by Kristen Proby
DAWN OF SURRENDER by Liliana Hart

COLLECTION FIVE
BLAZE ERUPTING by Rebecca Zanetti
ROUGH RIDE by Kristen Ashley
HAWKYN by Larissa Ione
RIDE DIRTY by Laura Kaye
ROME'S CHANCE by Joanna Wylde
THE MARRIAGE ARRANGEMENT by Jennifer Probst
SURRENDER by Elisabeth Naughton
INKED NIGHTS by Carrie Ann Ryan
ENVY by Rachel Van Dyken
PROTECTED by Lexi Blake
THE PRINCE by Jennifer L. Armentrout
PLEASE ME by J. Kenner
WOUND TIGHT by Lorelei James
STRONG by Kylie Scott
DRAGON NIGHT by Donna Grant
TEMPTING BROOKE by Kristen Proby
HAUNTED BE THE HOLIDAYS by Heather Graham
CONTROL by K. Bromberg
HUNKY HEARTBREAKER by Kendall Ryan
THE DARKEST CAPTIVE by Gena Showalter

Also from 1001 Dark Nights:

TAME ME by J. Kenner
THE SURRENDER GATE By Christopher Rice
SERVICING THE TARGET By Cherise Sinclair
TEMPT ME by J. Kenner

Discover More Lexi Blake

Protected: **A Masters and Mercenaries Novella by Lexi Blake**

A second chance at first love

Years before, Wade Rycroft fell in love with Geneva Harris, the smartest girl in his class. The rodeo star and the shy academic made for an odd pair but their chemistry was undeniable. They made plans to get married after high school but when Genny left him standing in the rain, he joined the Army and vowed to leave that life behind. Genny married the town's golden boy, and Wade knew that he couldn't go home again.

Could become the promise of a lifetime

Fifteen years later, Wade returns to his Texas hometown for his brother's wedding and walks into a storm of scandal. Genny's marriage has dissolved and the town has turned against her. But when someone tries to kill his old love, Wade can't refuse to help her. In his years after the Army, he's found his place in the world. His job at McKay-Taggart keeps him happy and busy but something is missing. When he takes the job watching over Genny, he realizes what it is.

As danger presses in, Wade must decide if he can forgive past sins or let the woman of his dreams walk into a nightmare…

* * * *

Close Cover: **A Masters and Mercenaries Novel by Lexi Blake**

Remy Guidry doesn't do relationships. He tried the marriage thing once, back in Louisiana, and learned the hard way that all he really needs in life is a cold beer, some good friends, and the occasional hookup. His job as a bodyguard with McKay-Taggart gives him purpose and lovely perks, like access to Sanctum. The last thing he needs in his life is a woman with stars in her eyes and babies in her future.

Lisa Daley's life is finally going in the right direction. She has finally graduated from college after years of putting herself through school. She's got a new job at an accounting firm and she's finished her Sanctum training. Finally on her own and having fun, her life seems pretty perfect. Except she's lonely and the one man she wants won't give her a second look.

There is one other little glitch. Apparently, her new firm is really a front for the mob and now they want her dead. Assassins can really ruin a fun girls' night out. Suddenly strapped to the very same six-foot-five-inch hunk of a bodyguard who makes her heart pound, Lisa can't decide if this situation is a blessing or a curse.

As the mob closes in, Remy takes his tempting new charge back to the safest place he knows—his home in the bayou. Surrounded by his past, he can't help wondering if Lisa is his future. To answer that question, he just has to keep her alive.

* * * *

Arranged: A Masters and Mercenaries Novella by **Lexi Blake**

Kash Kamdar is the king of a peaceful but powerful island nation. As Loa Mali's sovereign, he is always in control, the final authority. Until his mother uses an ancient law to force her son into marriage. His prospective queen is a buttoned-up intellectual, nothing like Kash's usual party girl. Still, from the moment of their forced engagement, he can't stop thinking about her.

Dayita Samar comes from one of Loa Mali's most respected families. The Oxford-educated scientist has dedicated her life to her country's future. But under her staid and calm exterior, Day hides a few sexy secrets of her own. She is willing to marry her king, but also agrees that they can circumvent the law. Just because they're married doesn't mean they have to change their lives. It certainly doesn't mean they have to fall in love.

After one wild weekend in Dallas, Kash discovers his bride-to-be is more than she seems. Engulfed in a changing world, Kash finds exciting new possibilities for himself. Could Day help him find respite from the crushing responsibility he's carried all his life? This fairy tale could have a happy ending, if only they can escape Kash's past...

* * * *

Dungeon Games: A Masters and Mercenaries Novella by Lexi Blake

Obsessed

Derek Brighton has become one of Dallas's finest detectives through a combination of discipline and obsession. Once he has a target in his sights, nothing can stop him. When he isn't solving homicides, he applies the same intensity to his playtime at Sanctum, a secretive BDSM club. Unfortunately, no amount of beautiful submissives can fill the hole that one woman left in his heart.

Unhinged

Karina Mills has a reputation for being reckless, and her clients appreciate her results. As a private investigator, she pursues her cases with nothing holding her back. In her personal life, Karina yearns for something different. Playing at Sanctum has been a safe way to find peace, but the one Dom who could truly master her heart is out of reach.

Enflamed

On the hunt for a killer, Derek enters a shadowy underworld only to find the woman he aches for is working the same case. Karina is searching for a missing girl and won't stop until she finds her. To get close to their prime suspect, they need to pose as a couple. But as their operation goes under the covers, unlikely partners become passionate lovers while the killer prepares to strike.

* * * *

Adored: A Masters and Mercenaries Novella by Lexi Blake

A man who gave up on love

Mitch Bradford is an intimidating man. In his professional life, he has a reputation for demolishing his opponents in the courtroom. At the exclusive BDSM club Sanctum, he prefers disciplining pretty submissives with no strings attached. In his line of work, there's no time for a healthy relationship. After a few failed attempts, he knows he's not good for any woman—especially not his best friend's sister.

A woman who always gets what she wants

Laurel Daley knows what she wants, and her sights are set on Mitch. He's smart and sexy, and it doesn't matter that he's a few years older and has a couple of bitter ex-wives. Watching him in action at work and at play, she knows he just needs a little polish to make some woman the perfect lover. She intends to be that woman, but first she has to show him how good it could be.

A killer lurking in the shadows

When an unexpected turn of events throws the two together, Mitch and Laurel are confronted with the perfect opportunity to explore their mutual desire. Night after night of being close breaks down Mitch's defenses. The more he sees of Laurel, the more he knows he wants her. Unfortunately, someone else has their eyes on Laurel and they have murder in mind.

* * * *

Devoted: A Masters and Mercenaries Novella by Lexi Blake

A woman's work

Amy Slaten has devoted her life to Slaten Industries. After ousting her corrupt father and taking over the CEO role, she thought she could relax and enjoy taking her company to the next level. But an old business rivalry rears its ugly head. The only thing that can possibly take her mind off business is the training class at Sanctum…and her training partner, the gorgeous and funny Flynn Adler. If she can just manage to best her mysterious business rival, life might be perfect.

A man's commitment

Flynn Adler never thought he would fall for the enemy. Business is war, or so his father always claimed. He was raised to be ruthless when it came to the family company, and now he's raising his brother to one day work with him. The first order of business? The hostile takeover of Slaten Industries. It's a stressful job so when his brother offers him a spot in Sanctum's training program, Flynn jumps at the chance.

A lifetime of devotion….

When Flynn realizes the woman he's falling for is none other than the CEO of the firm he needs to take down, he has to make a choice. Does he take care of the woman he's falling in love with or the business he's worked a lifetime to build? And when Amy finally understands the man she's come to trust is none other than the enemy, will she walk away from him or fight for the love she's come to depend on?

Lost in You

Masters and Mercenaries: The Forgotten, Book 3
By Lexi Blake
Coming August 6, 2019

Robert McClellan was forced to serve as a soldier in a war he didn't understand. Liberated by McKay-Taggart, he struggles every day to reclaim the life he lost and do right by the men he calls his brothers, The Lost Boys. Only one thing is more important – Ariel Adisa. The gorgeous psychologist has plagued his dreams since the day they met. Even as their mission pushes him to his limits, he can't stop thinking about taking his shot at finding a life beyond all this with her.

Ariel Adisa is a force to be reckoned with. Her performance in Toronto proved she's more than just a brilliant mind, but Robert still acts as if she is a wilting flower who needs his protection. Joining him on the mission to Munich should be the perfect opportunity to test their skills and cement their relationship. She and Robert are an excellent match. But when a stunning secret from Robert's past is revealed, their world is turned upside down and nothing will ever be the same again.

While they chase dark secrets across Europe, Robert and Ariel realize that the only thing worse than not knowing who you are could be discovering who you used to be...

* * * *

"Are you all right?" Ariel had stopped beside him. "Is Dante giving you trouble?"

He was glad she'd been upstairs when they'd gone on their rant. "I think the pressure is starting to get to him. But we can talk about that tomorrow. I think after we get back to London we should have a big group meeting and get some things out in the open."

"They think Damon and Ian are keeping things from them?"

No. He did not want to go there. He stopped in the middle of the hall and got into her personal space. She backed up against the wall and he loomed over her. It was time to move from reality to a place where they might be able to play out a few fantasies, if she was ready. "No work talk. If you want to go to sleep, I'll kiss you now and see you in the morning. Tucker and I are in the room next to you. If you need anything I'll be there. If you aren't tired and you want to talk some more, we can go down to the bar and have another glass of wine with the full knowledge we don't have to go any further than that. I'm more than willing to sit up talking to you all night long."

She tilted to her head up to him. "And if I want to go to bed but not to sleep?"

His heart rate ticked up, blood starting to thrum through his system as he invaded further, brushing his chest against hers. He reached for her wrists and gently brought them up and over her head, pinning her to the wall. "Then we need to make a few things clear."

She took a deep breath, her lips curling up as though she liked the way he smelled. "Me sub, you Dom. Got it."

He leaned over. "Hey, I'm trying to make sure I take care of you the way you like to be taken care of. I've watched you play. I don't think your play partners realized how much you like being dominated. I think they view you as a woman who enjoys a spanking from time to time. They don't get how much you need to know your partner is thinking about how to handle you. They don't understand that you need to stop thinking. You need a place where you obey your partner."

"In their defense, I had no interest in sex with any of them. I was looking for a spanking, some physical play that wouldn't lead to real intimacy. You watched me?"

"I always watch you," he admitted. "It's why my brothers insist I'm your stalker. I watch you because I can't not watch you when you're in a room. If I thought for a second that it made you uncomfortable, I would make myself stop, but I think you like it."

She watched him, too, and not in a way that made him think she was wary of him. It had always been there between them—the crackle and fire of sexual chemistry.

"You're going to be a talky one, aren't you?" she asked.

And she was going to be a brat. "You're the one who usually makes everyone else do the talking. Yes, I want you to talk to me. I want you to tell me how you're feeling and if the things I'm going to do to your body work for you. I need you to understand that nothing is more important to me for the rest of the night than ensuring that you're well taken care of. So let's set some ground rules. Unless you want me to play this vanilla. I can do that. I can very gently take you inside and lay you out on the bed and then I'll make love to you."

Her eyes flared. "Or you could bend me to your will and fuck me so hard I can't think of anything or anyone but you."

He liked how she thought. "Then stop being a brat. And yes, I'm a talkie top. I'll make you talk to me while we're playing. This is my therapy session, Dr. Adisa. You're not in charge. Say that. Tell me who's in charge."

"You are, Robert." Her tone had softened along with her eyes.

"And who obeys me?"

"I do. I obey you when we're playing."

"Tell me your safe word." He had no intention of her using it, but they needed it there between them.

"I've always used red, but I'm not going to use it with you."

"But you have it if you need it. We're going to walk into that room and you're going to strip for me. You're going to present yourself to me. Am I understood?"

Her pupils had dilated and her body seemed more languid than it had before. Him taking control was doing exactly what he'd thought it would.

"Yes, Sir."

"Then kiss me sweetly and do what I commanded."

She popped up on her toes and brushed her lips against his. Heat flashed through him and he had the overwhelming need to press her against the wall and find a place between her legs. He could shove his cock inside her and not stop until they both came.

Or he could make this last for a very long time. He could spend hours and hours playing with her because making love to Ariel wouldn't merely be about an orgasm.

About Lexi Blake

Lexi Blake is the author of contemporary and urban fantasy romance. She started publishing in 2011 and has gone on to sell over two million copies of her books. Her books have appeared twenty-six times on the *USA Today*, *New York Times*, and *Wall Street Journal* bestseller lists. She lives in North Texas with her husband, kids, and two rescue dogs.

Connect with Lexi online:

Facebook: Lexi Blake
Twitter: authorlexiblake
Website: www.LexiBlake.net
Instagram: www.instagram.com/lexi4714

On behalf of 1001 Dark Nights,

Liz Berry and M.J. Rose would like to thank ~

Steve Berry
Doug Scofield
Kim Guidroz
Jillian Stein
InkSlinger PR
Dan Slater
Asha Hossain
Chris Graham
Chelle Olson
Kasi Alexander
Jessica Johns
Dylan Stockton
Richard Blake
and Simon Lipskar